THE WISH RIDER

Barbara Casey

An imprint of Gauthier Publications

Gauthier Publications
P.O. Box 806241
Saint Clair Shores, MI 48080
Attention Permissions Department

This is a work of fiction. All characters in this book are fictitious and any similarities are coincidence and unintentional.

1st Edition
Proudly printed and bound in the USA
Hungry Goat Press is an Imprint of Gauthier Publications
www.EATaBOOK.com

Cover Artwork: Daniel J. Gauthier
Book Design: Elizabeth Gauthier

Book 2 of the F.I.G Mysteries

Library of Congress information on file

If wishes were horses
Beggars would ride:
If turnips were bayonets
I would wear one by my side.

James Carmichaell,
Collection of Proverbs in Scots

To Sophia Belle

With my love

CHAPTER ONE

*A*nyone can vanish. Maybe it is because they get lost, or they get abducted, or maybe they get killed. Or maybe they just want to leave the place where they are and the people they know and not ever be found again. These were the thoughts running through the mind of Dara Roux as she lay in her bed with the covers pulled neatly around her, staring into the darkness and listening to the faint ticking of the clock next to her bed. Then, as always whenever she faced an especially challenging situation or her thoughts became too heavy—a bit too serious, she focused on a foreign language, first establishing the root of each main word, or symbol in some cases, and assigning it a certain "weight" or number. By knowing this, she could then figure out the origin of the word; and from that, it was just a short step to recognizing its meaning. It was her own system, something she taught herself as a young African American child living with her mother in the back-bay area of Richmond, Virginia. From the age of two, she could speak and write seven languages, including the ancient language of Sanskrit, and she had an understanding of the characters from an obsolete Chinese dialect as well as Egyptian hieroglyphics. Now, as an eighteen year old and a new graduate of Wood Rose Orphanage and Academy for Young Women in Raleigh, North Carolina, that list had grown to forty-two languages and a smattering of the unusual such as the Dead Sea Scrolls and Geechee, a distinctive language spoken by the descendants of enslaved Africans living in the low country region of South Carolina and Georgia.

On this particular night, though, as she attempted to turn away from thoughts about vanishing, she focused on an ancient dialect of the Romani New Indo-Aryan language with its Greek, Iranian, Kurdish and Armenian influences. It was the language of the gypsies, and something which she had become familiar with only just recently.

The ability to translate any language, ancient or otherwise, and make it her own private language was how Dara's mind functioned. It had always been that way. It was what helped her to survive when she and her mother had nothing to eat; and then later, after her mother vanished and Dara wound up living in orphanages. It was what made her a genius. Now, in the darkness of her room, the possibility of actually finding her mother after ten long years weighed heavily on her mind, and it was the language of gypsies that she turned to.

She glanced at the soft green illuminated numbers of the clock; it was 2 a.m.—"witches' moments" she had heard Jimmy Bob Doake, the night watchman at Wood Rose, call it—the magical time that occurs between late darkness and early light. It was the third night in a row that she hadn't been able to sleep. The third night since she and her two best friends, Mackenzie Yarborough and Jennifer Torres, also orphans with intelligence quotients in the genius range, along with their teacher and mentor, Carolina Lovel, had returned from Frascati, Italy. That was where after years of wondering and searching, Carolina found her own mother—a gypsy.

It was amazing, really, that so much had happened in such a short period of time—Carolina getting hired at Wood Rose, the mysterious Voynich Manuscript, Mother and Papa Granchelli, the Villa Mondragone, the *Kaulo Camioes* or Black Gypsies. And even before all of that, the fact that three orphans with intelligence quotients in the genius range, each coming from different parts of the country, would wind up at the same orphanage in North Carolina was remarkable in itself.

What the three of them had managed to do to the headmaster's bush was pretty amazing as well, the bush that he had personally fertilized and watered, treated for a rare mold disease, nursed back to health from an equally rare fungus, and hand-trimmed weekly since first planting it when he was named headmaster at Wood Rose. Of course, the three young women, or FIGs—Females of Intellectual Genius as they were called at Wood Rose Orphanage and Academy for Young Women—were known for their "expressions of creativity" whenever things got boring or less than stimulating for them at the orphanage, so it hadn't surprised anyone. In fact, these expressions had occurred quite often and with regularity until Carolina, only a few years older than the FIGs, with outstanding educational credentials and an open mind, a friendly personality and quiet demeanor, and the one person on campus the FIGs took an immediate liking to, was hired to be responsible for the three brilliant girls—their education, their social development, and, in short, keeping them out of trouble.

But even with Carolina's guidance and realistic, grounded sense of maintaining a proper perspective when it related to the FIGs, and her herculean efforts in keeping them "engaged" in worthwhile studies and activities, they still, occasionally, the three young women—Dara, Mackenzie, and Jennifer—felt the overwhelming need to creatively express themselves. And it was out of this need that in their last expression they had managed, in the middle of the night—the "witches' moments," to prune the headmaster's prize red-tip bush, his 14-foot tall *Photinia frasen,* to a magnificent, perfectly shaped, phallic symbol. The FIGs immediately named it *Peni erecti.*

It was this type of expression of creativity that tended to keep the girls in a state of bad grace at Wood Rose, and in particular with Headmaster Thurgood James Harcourt, not to mention the other faculty and staff. It was only Jimmy Bob who seemed to be oblivious, and left untouched and unperturbed by their actions as he maintained his own steadfast routine of keeping all within the ivy-covered walls of the orphanage safe.

It was the Sunday morning after that creative expression involving the headmaster's bush when Carolina invited the three girls to her cottage, following breakfast at 8:30 and mandatory chapel service from 10 until 11. They expected to be reprimanded, or even worse. As Mackenzie pointed out, "Maybe this time we have gone too far—what if Carolina got fired because of *Pen... Pen... Peni erecti?*" stumbling a little bit on the word *Peni* because she had the tendency to have a lisp whenever she became anxious or upset.

They were not reprimanded, and Carolina had not lost her job. Instead, she had fixed them all coffee, with cream for Dara and Jennifer, and sugar for Mackenzie. After getting each of them to agree to write the headmaster a note of apology, she said, "I have a story to tell you," in her soft-spoken voice, her dark hair casually swept up off her neck with a clip, wearing jeans and a tee shirt, and looking very much like a student herself. It was then that she showed them the small wooden box—her "special project" she described it. And it was from that moment that Carolina took the FIGs on the most amazing adventure of their young lives, traveling to Frascati, Italy, in search of her connection to the *Kaulo Camioes*—the Black Gypsy tribe, and the most mysterious document in the world—the Voynich Manuscript.

Larry Gitani, Carolina's boyfriend, followed them to Frascati just in case they needed his help, and it was there that he revealed he was the son of a Gypsy King. That was when Dara decided to ask him if he could help her find her own mother who had simply vanished when Dara was only seven years old. The day after graduating from Wood Rose, Larry told Dara that based on what he had uncovered, her mother might be in New York City, and he gave her some information that could be useful in locating her.

With graduation now behind them, and a few weeks left before each FIG was to report to the university where she would be attending that fall, Jennifer and Mackenzie were planning to go to New York with Dara, as was Carolina. For the three FIGs considered Carolina one of them, and it just wouldn't feel right if she couldn't be with them.

Of course, Carolina needed to get permission from the headmaster first since the FIGs were still considered part of the

Wood Rose community until they officially left at the end of summer, and she was meeting him first thing after breakfast. Which was why Dara had been unable to sleep the past three nights, why she was thinking about the ancient dialect of the Romani New Indo-Aryan language with its Greek, Iranian, Kurdish and Armenian influences, and why she was feeling so challenged—stoic; but challenged. The "What If" game which brought doubt bubbling to the surface was interfering with the ancient gypsy words she was trying to translate in her mind.

What If I can't find my mother?
What If I do find my mother, but she doesn't want to see me?
What If she really did vanish?
What If... I am just a beggar riding a wish?

***

All of her life Mackenzie had been afraid. She had been afraid of saying the wrong thing, of doing the wrong thing, and that by not living up to someone else's expectations—it didn't matter whose they were—she wouldn't be adopted. So she focused on the one thing she enjoyed the most that caused the least amount of criticism. Even at a very young age, that focus was on numbers. She loved them—playing with them, seeing how many unusual ways she could make them relate to each other and how they could relate to her. In some ways, numbers became her friends. It was a mechanism of self-protection she had invented from the time she was able to talk and what she did to create safe boundaries around herself so she wouldn't get hurt. Then, at age seven, because of her obvious exceptional mathematical skills and proclivity toward solving difficult puzzles, she was transferred from the orphanage in upstate New York that had been her home since birth to Wood Rose Orphanage and Academy for Young Women in Raleigh, North Carolina. That was where another seven year old child, this one with exceptional abilities

5

in foreign languages, had also only recently been admitted. The other child was Dara Roux, Mackenzie soon learned, and the two quickly became inseparable, each sensing the other's needs as only two girls with brilliance could.

When they turned nine years old, the age when the possibility for adoption drops by 85 percent, Mackenzie's old fear of failure was replaced by a new fear. This was the fear of not fitting in with the other girls at Wood Rose who also had not been chosen to live with a forever family. Dara, who was a lot taller than the other girls her age, wasn't afraid of anything, though, and when Mackenzie told her of her new fear, she was quick to console her. "Who wants to be put in a family with all those rules?" reasoned Dara. "You wouldn't be able to do anything—not like we can do here."

Still, Mackenzie had already calculated that being one kid out of 38 under the watchful eye of 15 Wood Rose faculty members and 25 members of the staff and administration didn't increase the odds in her favor that much of being able to do whatever she wanted. But, with Dara as her best friend, this fear also diminished over time, and her lisp only became pronounced in situations that caused extreme nervousness and anxiety.

Strangely enough, just a few years later a third orphan—a young girl from the northern part of Connecticut, with exceptional abilities in music and art, was admitted to Wood Rose. Her name was Jennifer Torres, and her parents had been killed in an automobile accident. In just a short time, her brilliance was recognized by Dara and Mackenzie, and she became accepted by them.

It was at Wood Rose that Mackenzie broadened her focus to include calculus, algebra, algorithms, geometry, and numerical codes. And when she reached her teen years and realized that the probability of her ever being adopted had dropped to less than one percent, Dara convinced her that they were too old for a family anyway. After all, the three of them—Dara, Mackenzie, and Jennifer—were the FIGs. They were Females of Intellectual

Genius, and they could accomplish anything they set out to do, Dara told her confidently. And they had each other—which was the same thing as having a family anyway only better. Especially when Carolina came. For she was also one of them, and she openly and willingly included them into her life; loving and accepting them for who they were, and sharing her own fears and vulnerabilities.

Mackenzie lay curled up in a ball, bed sheets twisted around her and spilling onto the floor, running mathematical formulae through her mind. Because of her special talent in the field of physics, calculus, computers, and problem-solving—especially in the area of complex geometrical puzzles—she was mentally preparing a grid using special equations that pinpointed each address of the women Larry had identified who might be Dara's mother. There were five of them. Visualizing a probability equation in one quadrant, and using the Law of Sufficient Reason, she was hoping to be able to determine which of the women could most likely be Dara's mother. Unable to sleep, this was how she occupied herself.

With the final address inserted into its proper slot on the grid, she rolled over, twisting the sheets even more, and glanced at the clock, which was identical to Dara's and Jennifer's, as were their rooms; for they shared a three-bedroom suite on the second floor of the dormitory that housed the older residents. The green numbers on the clock told her it was 2 a.m. She tried to think of other ways she could help Dara find her mother, assuming Thurgood would give Carolina permission to take them to New York over the summer. Feeling a little anxious, and because being a little on the heavy side she had a tendency to be warm-blooded, she stuck one leg out from under the crumpled dark blue sheet and light-weight summer blanket like a barometer.

Everything at Wood Rose was dark blue and yellow, including their uniforms, their bed linens and bathroom towels and washcloths, as well as their upholstered furniture and rugs. At the end of summer, however, Dara, Jennifer, and Mackenzie would each be going to different universities in order to pursue their specialties, and they would be able to choose any color they wanted for their clothes and dormitory furnishings.

She considered the color orange, or maybe purple. The school colors at the Massachusetts Institute of Technology where she would be attending in the fall were red and gray—perhaps those colors would do. Then she turned her thoughts to all that had happened leading up to the three FIGs graduating from Wood Rose a few days earlier.

Carolina had taken them to Frascati, Italy, so they could help her find out about her birth parents; for, like the FIGs, Carolina was also an orphan—something she had learned when she turned eighteen. They had stayed with a wonderful elderly couple, Signor and Signora Granchelli, on their farm which had chickens and cows and a vineyard. It was Mackenzie's job to collect the eggs each morning and then help prepare breakfast. It was the first "real" home she had ever been in; the first time she had experienced what it was like to be part of a true family—not just the little family of the FIGs and Carolina. She had never known such happiness.

The farm was situated several kilometers off the main road that ran between the village of Frascati and the ancient Villa Mondragone where Carolina, Dara, Mackenzie, and Jennifer did their research. That was also where Mackenzie met Alfonso, Rector Catoni's young assistant—"a hottie," Dara described him—who looked after the young women each day while at the Villa Mondragone. "The name *Alfonso* is derived from Visigothic *Adalfuns*," Dara had told Mackenzie and Jennifer with an arched right eyebrow, "and it means noble—and ready," causing the other two FIGs to giggle.

The Granchellis treated each of them like their own children, taking care of them, especially when Carolina got so sick, and giving them the kind of parental love and attention they had never experienced. By the time they left to return to Wood Rose, Mackenzie felt as though she had another family—first there was Dara and Jennifer and Carolina, then Signor and Signora Granchelli—"Mother Granchelli and Papa," the young women had called them.

Alfonso had promised to write to her as well just as soon as she got settled at MIT where she would be involved in a special research program. An anonymous donor and Miss Alcott, the great niece of the founding father of Wood Rose who was one of the major financial supporters, were sponsoring her. She giggled now wondering how she would be able to read his letters since he only knew Italian and she only knew English. But she could always depend on Dara to translate them for her; that is, if Dara wasn't too busy at Yale University where she had been accepted on a full scholarship. Dara wanted to continue her studies in foreign languages and perhaps at some point go into the diplomatic service. And Jennifer had been accepted at Juilliard where she would continue her advanced studies in art and music except when she was performing internationally.

Dara was not only the tallest of the other girls her age at Wood Rose, she was also the most outgoing. And of the three FIGs, she was the strongest both mentally and emotionally— she always had been. Now, however, facing the possibility of finding her mother, Mackenzie wondered if Dara perhaps felt a little anxious—like she did. After all, Dara was just left in that store and her mother never came back for her. What if something terrible had happened to her mother, or, what if she just didn't want Dara to find her because she didn't love her? And, of course, there was also the worry that Thurgood might not even let them go to New York.

Mackenzie flipped the crumpled dark blue covers off the bed into a pile on the floor and climbed out. Trying not to wake Jennifer, she quietly tiptoed into Dara's room, carefully walking near the walls in order to avoid the three floorboards in the middle of the room that always creaked. "Dara? Are you asleep?" The word "asleep" sounded a little like "astheep" because she was feeling slightly worried and anxious.

"No!"

Dara carefully folded back the covers and let her friend climb into the bed with her. The two friends, laying side by side, feet touching, stared into the darkness, their brilliant minds filled with the language of gypsies and mathematical grids, anxiously awaiting breakfast and the meeting that would take place immediately afterwards.

***

It had started again. Just like always. The feeling like there was a large, heavy stone in her chest. Soon the black and white images—like charcoal drawings—would appear in her mind's eye, later changing to color. Eventually, the beats would start— hesitant at first, then becoming insistent—refusing to be ignored. Just as the cadence had started beating in Jennifer's mind the moment she saw the Voynich Manuscript, it was beating now, once again, as she lay in bed, in the darkness of her room.

Considered a wild child, Jennifer Torres was a musical prodigy from the age of two. She had kept her parents in a state of exhaustion with her sudden and unexplained emotional outbursts followed by days of deep depression. A long list of pediatricians was consulted, along with an equally long list of different drugs prescribed, but Jennifer remained a child who could not and would not be controlled. Public schools were out of the question; she had to be taught by private tutoring.

By the time she reached the age of puberty, she had composed a four-movement symphony for full orchestra, a fugue that she had also transcribed into a rondo, numerous individual pieces that focused on two or three single instruments such as the piano, violin and cello, and a piano sonata. It was the sonata that gained her world-wide prominence when she performed it at Carnegie Hall over Thanksgiving the year she turned 13.

After that, the temper tantrums and bouts with depression became less frequent for a while, and her parents began to travel to Europe. Sometimes they would take Jennifer. As long as she had her portfolio filled with blank, eight-stave paper with her in which she could write down the music that filled her very being, then things might be all right. But not always. There were still problems and, often, embarrassing moments when Jennifer couldn't be stopped from acting out. Gradually, Jennifer's parents began leaving her behind with an assortment of hired help. They were escaping from her and her unpredictable behavior, and Jennifer knew it. They didn't know how to control her, any more than she knew how to control herself.

Ironically, it was when they had returned from a trip to England and had gone to the neighborhood grocery store for a few items when the accident occurred. Both were killed instantly. There were no close relatives, at least none who were willing to take on the responsibility of caring for such an unpredictable, emotional child. So with a little less than two years to go before she could be considered an adult and allowed to live on her own, Jennifer was placed in the Wood Rose Orphanage and Academy for Young Women. They had an excellent music department and art department, both nationally recognized, she was assured, where she could continue her studies.

The "excellent" music and art departments, however, weren't prepared for Jennifer. At 16 years of age she possessed more talent than the six faculty members making up the two departments put together. It would have been a disaster if it hadn't been for Dara and Mackenzie. Like Jennifer, they also were considered different—because they were. They understood what it was like to try to communicate on a level where others would understand, but not succeed. To want to be included, but feeling resentful because they couldn't be. To want desperately to be like everyone else, but knowing that was impossible—because they weren't and never would be. And, as Dara said repeatedly, it just didn't matter anyway!

With the arrival of Jennifer, the strong union between Mackenzie and Dara was stretched to include this strange, petite girl who was either poised for battle or locked in a silent world of musical notes. It had been only Dara and Mackenzie for so long. But even as different as Jennifer was, or maybe because of it, they could each still relate to the other; she fit in. They shared the common goal of trying to survive in an environment where they were considered odd, their behavior, strange. Therefore, within a short time, the "new girl" also became Mackenzie's and Dara's friend. When her temper raged out of control, it was Dara who could calm her. When she needed space and solitude because the pictures filling her mind had changed into so many musical notes that she couldn't write them down fast enough, Mackenzie understood and protected her.

For a while, they just had each other—the three of them—until Carolina arrived. Instinctively they knew Carolina was one of them. They sensed her empathy and understanding—her acceptance—and her genuine love and concern for them. In return, they accepted her, and they loved her for it.

Within days after Carolina's arrival on campus, it was determined that because of Jennifer's exceptional musical and artistic talents, she also should be Carolina's responsibility and included in the small class with Dara and Mackenzie. This decision was reached with full approval and much relief of the entire Wood Rose faculty.

Since each of the girls had an extremely high intelligence quotient, it was a little daunting to Carolina when she was first told that she and she alone would be responsible for their education and generally looking after them. "Keeping them on a short leash" was the phrase Headmaster Harcourt used. The FIGs were, after all, the brightest students at Wood Rose; in fact, they were in the top two percent of the entire population according to their intelligence quotient scores which reached above 200, putting them in a category of profoundly gifted and their genius unmeasurable. "They seem to listen to you, Ms. Lovel," Dr. Harcourt had explained. "It is obvious, for whatever reason, you are able to inspire them where some—most—of the other faculty members have"—there was a deep sigh—"not succeeded. Therefore, I am putting you in charge of these three girls. I trust you will not fail them—or Wood Rose."

Jennifer had now been at Wood Rose for not quite a year, perhaps considered a short time for some, but not for most who called the orphanage home due to circumstances over which they had no control, and certainly not for Jennifer. Small-framed, blond, and still thought of as the new girl by the other two FIGs, Jennifer had felt the pain, like a massive rock in her chest, for as long as she could remember, even before her parents' death. Since moving to Wood Rose, however, the rock had started to get smaller, the pain not so severe, especially with Carolina's arrival. In fact, other than when that mean gypsy boy put the curse on Carolina, even with all of the exciting events of the past several weeks in Italy, there had been hardly any sign of it at all. The drawings and the musical notes had been there for *The Gypsy Cadence,* but the pain she associated with the rock had been only slight.

She wasn't sure what the pain meant or where it came from; only, like before whenever a new musical composition was forming in her mind, it came first, followed by a black and white image—like a charcoal drawing. Over time the image would gradually change to color; and along with the color would come a beat—the cadence she called it; first softly, then pronounced, loud—*fortissimo*, demanding, and vibrating. It was then that she knew she needed to capture its musical essence. This was when she wrote the notes on eight-stave musical paper, composing them as she heard them in her mind. That was her genius.

But the images and the notes would come later. Right now, there was only the pain, and she was certain it had to do with going to New York and looking for Dara's mother. For her, there would never be a search for her parents. She knew her parents were dead. But for Dara, there was that hope—and the FIGs and Carolina would do everything they could to help Dara and see that her wish was fulfilled.

Of course, there was still old man Harcourt to get around, but Carolina knew how to handle him. If everything went as planned, the four of them—Dara, Mackenzie, Jennifer, and Carolina—would be on their way to New York very soon. And once in New York, they would find Dara's mother. Then, at the end of summer, before returning to Wood Rose and before each FIG went her separate way, Jennifer would be reintroduced to the international world of music and perform once again at Carnegie Hall, something she had done when she had played her piano sonata at the age of thirteen. This time she would perform as principal violinist with a full orchestra *The Gypsy Cadence*. It was the symphony she had written while they were in Italy, created out of the pain, the black and white images that changed to color, and finally the music that filled her very soul.

Now, in the quiet of her room, Jennifer shifted slightly against her pillow as though to test it. The pain was still there, but it had eased. Because of her strong artistic nature, Jennifer was also the most sensitive of the three FIGs and most in tune to what other people were feeling. She knew the uncertainty Dara must be feeling now, just as she knew that Mackenzie was afraid and self-conscious. Climbing out of her bed, she went into Dara's room, walking across the creaking floorboards in the middle of the room, not caring if they squeaked or not.

"Come on," said Dara, as though she had expected her. "You might as well get in bed with us, too." Without saying anything, Jennifer squeezed next to her two best friends, being careful not to mess up the neatly folded sheets because she knew that was the way Dara liked them, touching a foot with one of hers, reaching for a hand, and staring into the darkness. Only the soft ticking of the clock interrupted the silence…

…until, suddenly Dara sat up and threw back the covers. "*Shekoo, baboo!*" an obvious expletive from a foreign language or some unknown tongue. "Come on, we need to be creative."

Mackenzie giggled, sat up and fluffed her short brown hair confidently, then, with less confidence, said, "Are you sure, Dara?"

But Dara and Jennifer had already left their three-bedroom suite. Barefooted and wearing nothing but their dark blue pajamas with yellow piping, in Dara's and Mackenzie's case—a dark blue night shirt also with yellow piping in Jennifer's, the three FIGs tiptoed down to the end of the hall, past the other residents' suites, past the hall monitors' rooms, and past the apartment of their dorm mother, Ms. Larkins. There, after untying the string that was connected to a small bell in Ms. Larkins' bedroom—the dorm mother's homemade, somewhat crude, simplistic alarm system she had devised specifically because of the FIGs—they quietly pushed open the window and climbed out one by one onto the second-story roof. From there they slid down the drain pipe until reaching the expansive lawn, wet with dew, shadowed with tall pines and massive oaks draped in Spanish moss, and slightly illuminated by the quarter moon overhead. Jimmy Bob Doake, the night watchman, would be finished making his rounds in his old pickup truck and back in his room, probably watching a baseball game he had taped earlier on television.

All was as it should be at Wood Rose Orphanage and Academy for Young Women.

CHAPTER TWO

Carolina poured her third cup of coffee and sat back down at the small oak kitchen table—an antique shop find—littered with the papers Larry had given her. She had been up since 2 a.m. knowing she wasn't going to be able to sleep from worrying about her meeting with Headmaster Harcourt that was scheduled right after breakfast. To calm her nerves, she started thinking about her small wooden box—her "special project" she had always called it.

It had been given to her on her eighteenth birthday by Loraine and Ted Branson; the people Carolina had grown up believing to be her parents. That was also when she learned that she had been adopted when she was barely three years old, and part of the agreement was that she be given the box and its contents on the day she turned eighteen years old.

She didn't share her box with anyone for the longest time, preferring to keep it to herself like a secret priceless treasure. Eventually, though, she showed it to her boyfriend, Larry, because she needed his help to find out the meaning of some of the things in the box, and he was always so resourceful. Then, only recently, she had shared it with Dara, Mackenzie, and Jennifer—the FIGs—the three girls with intelligence quotients in the genius range that she had been given complete responsibility for at Wood Rose Orphanage and Academy for Young Women.

The contents of the box didn't seem like much at first. There was her birth certificate and some other documents from the adoption agency, and a faded black and white photograph of a dark-skinned man and woman. "That's when I learned what my true name is—Carolina Lovel, the daughter of Lyuba and Balo Lovel—and that my birth parents were gypsies," Carolina told

Dara, Mackenzie, and Jennifer that day in her bungalow. "So I changed my name from Branson to Lovel."

Carolina wanted them to know everything, so she told them about the history of the name. "Larry did some research and found out that the Lovel name is from an old and powerful English family. The gypsies who adopted it seem to have imagined that it had something to do with love for they translated it to *Camio* or *Caumio*, that which is lovely or amiable. *Camio* is connected with the Sanscrit *Cama,* which also signifies love, and is the appellation of the Hindoo god of love. If all tales be true, then those who are born by that divinity are black, which is perhaps why the gypsy tribe adopted it. The Lovel tribe is decidedly the darkest of all the Anglo-Egyptian families. They are generally called by the race the *Kaulo Camioes,* the Black Comelies." Each little bit of information had seemed so important, so revealing as Carolina peeled back the layers and learned who she was. And now she was telling the FIGs, hoping they would think it was important, too.

The FIGs were fascinated, especially Dara who immediately began assigning weights and numbers to the unfamiliar Romani words, determining their origin and meaning. Other than Jennifer who did remember her parents since she was sixteen when they were killed in an automobile accident, Mackenzie remembered nothing at all about her parents because she had been an infant when she was put in an orphanage, and Dara had been only seven when she was abandoned by her mother. A "late baby," she never knew her father or the much older siblings that had left home long before she was even born, so her memories were sketchy at best. For Carolina to reveal what she had gone through, to share with them how she felt when she found out she was adopted, and to let them examine her special treasures hidden away in a small wooden box was like giving each one of them permission to peep through a locked door and discover her own hidden past. "Now, this is where it gets interesting as far as you are concerned," Carolina told them. She was so excited to be sharing her special treasure with these special girls, and her excitement was contagious as the FIGs forgot their coffee and listened mesmerized. "There was a branch of Lovels that split from the original English tribe and settled in Italy, around the area of Frascati, where my birth certificate indicates I was born. I have been able to trace their origins as far back as the fourteenth century. There is a good possibility that they were around even before that, but instead of being known as gypsies back then, they were called land tramps. Of course I am not black—I have dark hair, but my eyes are green, and I have a pale complexion with freckles. But Signora De Rosa—Lucia, the woman who is head of the adoption agency in Frascati where I came from, explained that it is common knowledge that gypsies steal children—pretty children—usually in the community near where they are camped. But they also steal children from other gypsy tribes. It is a problem that continues even today," Carolina told her three charges, uncovering her story little by little. "Lucia also told me that there is a special unit within the *guardia di financa* who do nothing but search the gypsy camps for children who obviously do not have gypsy characteristics—such as green or blue eyes and fair complexions."

"What happens to the children?" asked Mackenzie.

"They are removed and placed into State custody. There are several published reasons for the removal of these children, the most common being *sfruttamento di minori."*

"Exploitation of minors," Dara translated.

"That is correct. If children are caught begging or selling knick-knacks either on their own or even in the presence of their parents, it is breaking the law. Truancy is another reason given. Mostly, gypsy children are taught within the camps where they live. Their parents do not trust outsiders and, therefore, do not allow their children to attend public schools. Also, unsanitary conditions might be used as a reason to remove a child from its gypsy parents."

"What happens to these children once they are in State custody?" asked Jennifer.

"Once the child is in State custody, it is rarely returned to the gypsy family. It is usually put up for adoption. So that could explain what happened to me and why I don't look like my birth parents." She smiled then and folded her hands in her lap. "Or, maybe it just happened—a white child born into the black tribe."

Carolina let the three FIGs examine the contents of the box. Also in the box was a small, colorful drawstring pouch that contained dried herbs, a small stone, a feather—from an owl she believed. "It is a gypsy *parik-til* or blessing holder," Carolina explained, something else she had learned from Larry. Then she told the FIGs that a savings account with fifty thousand dollars had been set up by her birth parents in her name at the time she was born. She held nothing back. The reason they got along so well was because of the trust they had for one another. Keeping that trust would only happen if she was completely open with them.

As the FIGs looked at the items one by one, touched them, became familiar with them, and understood how much these things meant to Carolina, it soon became clear that there was a mystery as to who Carolina's biological parents really were; but not until she told them about the Voynich Manuscript and showed them her copy of it did they realize just how much of a mystery it actually was. And how important it was to Carolina. "The original is seven by ten inches, about 235 pages long, and it's made of soft, light-brown vellum. Small, but thick. No one knows what the manuscript means," Carolina explained.

Mackenzie carefully looked through the strange book that had presented such a quandary for centuries, as one of her interests was solving complex geometrical puzzles. It appeared to be divided into five categories that included artwork in colors of red, blue, brown, yellow, and green which Jennifer was immediately drawn to since one of her specialties was art. "It is written from left to right, and the lines—they scan from the top of the page to the bottom," something that Dara was immediately interested in since her genius involved foreign languages. That was when Carolina revealed her greatest secret. "The style is a flowing cursive script in an alphabet that has never been seen elsewhere…" hesitating… "until now."

Engrossed in the manuscript pages spread out before them, with the unusual sections of text and colorful drawings, and comfortable in their surroundings of brightly-colored, hand-sewn cushions, slip covers and draperies, Carolina's admission first went unnoticed by the FIGs. Then everything became still.

Dara was the first to grasp the meaning of Carolina's words—or maybe it was the tone of her voice that she picked up on. It was then that Carolina showed them an old and creased single sheet of paper, yellowed with age, now carefully protected in clear, acid-free paper. She handed it to Dara. "This was folded up in the *parik-til*, in the box with my birth certificate. As soon as I saw it, I made the connection. It is the same script as the Voynich Manuscript—the most mysterious manuscript in the world."

The FIGs examined the paper that day in Carolina's cheerful little bungalow, light from the morning sun filtering through the hand-sewn draperies. Many of the symbols and words appeared to be the same as what was in the Voynich, perhaps even written by the same hand. "No one has ever been able to decipher or translate the Voynich Manuscript, although many scholars have tried," she told them, "but it is believed to be dated from the fifteenth century."

Carolina remembered how anxious she felt, waiting for her words to be absorbed by her three remarkable students—the FIGs: Dara Roux, abandoned when she was 7 years old by her mother, exceptionally gifted in foreign languages—orphan; Mackenzie Yarborough, no record of her parents or where she was born, exceptionally gifted in math and problem-solving—orphan; and Jennifer Torres, both parents killed in an automobile accident when she was 16, exceptionally gifted in music and art—orphan. Not knowing what else to say, or how to say it, Carolina refilled their cups with coffee, with sugar for Mackenzie, cream for Dara and Jennifer.

"The birth certificate indicates that I was born in Frascati, Italy. Strangely enough, it was also there, at the ancient Villa Mondragone, where the Voynich Manuscript was originally discovered." The three girls waited quietly, expectantly, for Carolina to continue. "I want to travel to Frascati to see if I can find out what the connection is between my paper and the most mysterious document in the world, and try to learn more about my birth parents," she told them. She also told them that she wanted the three of them to go with her.

She hoped they would understand this deep, driving need she had—something that had started the day she turned eighteen— and share her excitement, but was afraid they would think she was silly. The story she knew so well was a fascinating one, wrapped in mystery, adventure, and romance. It was her priceless treasure; her special project. As she told the story to them out loud, however, she wondered if it didn't sound a little ridiculous—like a young child's fantasy of finding a rare jewel, or discovering she wasn't an orphan after all but a princess. She had kept the secret of her treasure hidden for so long that now, bringing it out into the open, discussing it, and revealing it in this way was a little frightening, not to mention embarrassing.

She needn't have worried. Without hesitation the three FIGs all started talking at once. Of course they would go to Italy with Carolina. Dara could help with translations and, naturally, she spoke Italian fluently. Mackenzie could help organize everything once they actually started the research with her ability to analyze and solve problems as well as complex geometrical puzzles, and Jennifer could use her special talents in art and music to try to decipher the connection between the Voynich and Carolina's paper since sections of the Voynich were drawings. There was another reason Carolina wanted to take "her girls," as she called them, with her to Italy—a reason she thought it better not to mention—and that was to keep them out of trouble until the end of the school year when the three of them would graduate from Wood Rose. Headmaster Harcourt really was purple-faced upset about his bush and had been ready to suspend all three FIGs after what he considered a major, totally disrespectful, completely irreverent and vulgar infraction of rules involving his prized *Photinia frasen.* However, when Carolina presented her proposal to take the FIGs to Italy with her, at her expense, he had readily agreed; and from that moment on, the four young women set out on the most exciting adventure they had ever known.

And now it was Dara's turn.

From what Larry had been able to find out, there were five women with the name of Pearlee Devoraux Roux—Dara's mother's name—living in New York City, the last place Dara's mother was known to reside. How Larry was able to come up with even that much information in such a short period of time was a mystery to Carolina—except that he had always been able to do the impossible or find out the unknown. He was, after all, the son of a Gypsy King, a fact he had kept hidden from her until unexpectedly showing up in Italy when she and the FIGs were there. It was with Larry's help that she had been able to find her own mother.

Carolina sipped her coffee, thinking back to all she and the FIGs had accomplished in Italy. Of course, she had almost died from that curse the young gypsy boy, Milosh, placed on her. Mother and Papa Granchelli and the FIGs had taken care of her, though, and her mother, Lyuba, with Larry's help, had been able to break the curse and bring her back to good health.

That was when she learned that her father was dead and that her mother was a *choovihni* from the *Kaulo Camio* gypsy tribe—a wise woman who had been given the responsibility to pass on the ancient knowledge of the travelers to the ones who would follow. Knowing that about her mother made Carolina feel special—and happy. Her eyes suddenly filled with tears. Her mother was known as a "traveler" by some, a gypsy by others. Lyuba was of another world and time—something Carolina would never completely understand having been brought up in a different culture. She wasn't even sure if she would ever see her mother again, but just knowing who she was—the daughter of a *choovihni* with the blood of gypsies from the beginning of time running through her veins—and that her mother loved her—was enough. At least for now.

She was so proud of the FIGs—Dara, Mackenzie, and Jennifer. She would never have accomplished the task of finding her mother if they hadn't been with her giving their support, their intellectual genius, and their love. Now, by knowing where she came from and the circumstances leading to her adoption, the tear in her heart had been healed; the painful emptiness was no longer there. She wasn't Carolina Branson but Carolina Lovel, in name, in body, and in spirit, and that made her feel different—more confident and more alive. She was secure; and she felt whole. The need to rush everywhere for fear something had been left undone or unsaid was now gone. She was at peace, and she wanted the same thing for the FIGs, knowing they also had buried deep within them their own dreams and fantasies of what their parents were like had they known them, or, in Jennifer's case, if they had lived. She had done the same thing. It was a way of coping with knowing you were alone in the world; it was a way of trying to make something that was wrong right.

Carolina once again glanced through the papers in front of her—addresses, documents, maps, lists of other names that were possible contacts—letting her imagination take her to places where Dara might go in her own search. The information Larry had been able to find wasn't complete by any means, but he was so positive that one of the women on the list was Dara's mother. She only hoped that Dara wouldn't get hurt in her search. After all, Dara had been abandoned by her mother. Carolina couldn't understand how any mother could do that to her child, but maybe there had been a good reason, and regardless of the outcome, Carolina knew that Dara had no choice but to try to find her. Just as Carolina had no choice when she learned that she had been adopted. She had to face the psychic conflict between wanting primal familiarity or the search for novel experience. Familiarity was knowing and, more importantly, accepting without question who she was and her situation. The search for novel experience— her past, however, meant uncertainty, change, leaving the bounds of familiarity for something unknown. One was safe; the other, frightening. In the end, Carolina knew what she must do. The decision already had been made for her. She wanted to learn the truth. Without that, she would never feel complete as a person. Now that there was the possibility that Dara could find her mother and learn the truth, no matter what, she must try.

In Carolina's case, being told on her eighteenth birthday that she had been adopted answered a lot of questions for her, for she had never felt close to the Bransons, her adoptive parents. They had provided for her physical needs, and paid for her education, but the emotional warmth was lacking. She had grown up feeling envious of the loving family life her friends seemed to have. In her own family there was a distance, so much so that she felt like a visitor in her own home. With Dara, however, she was seven years old when her mother left her in that candy store, never to return. Dara was young, but she was still old enough to remember a few things. The old trailer they called home, set back off a dirt road near a ditch that usually flooded whenever it rained; the big black iron pot her mother burned kerosene in to keep the snakes away; a small garden, usually full of weeds. They didn't have much, from what Carolina gathered. The United States Navy owned the property nearby, protected by a chain-link fence in order to keep anyone out who didn't belong. What Carolina found especially interesting was the one thing Dara remembered most about her "mama" was her beautiful, red painted mouth.

Carolina walked into her small living room, taking the cup of coffee with her, and looked out the window. As a member of the faculty, she lived within the ivy-covered stone walls, on the orphanage property, in her own one-bedroom bungalow, something for which she gave thanks every day. Before coming to Wood Rose she had lived near the university campus in an efficiency apartment with shared walls, shared noises, and shared smells. Now she only had her own walls, her own noises, and her own smells which was a combination of fresh citrus and herbs, and whatever was in bloom which she had cut and brought indoors—a daffodil, a rose, perhaps a hydrangea.

The administration building was an unadorned three-story stone behemoth centered on sixty heavily-wooded acres of donated land. Radiating from the administration building in a semi-circle, much like the ribs of a fan, were two, two-story buildings, also built of stone. One contained the classrooms accommodating grades one through twelve. The other was the dormitory where thirty-eight orphans lived, ranging in age from 5 to 18. Each floor was divided into several spacious multi-roomed suites, the residents assigned according to class: elementary, grades one through six; middle, grades seven through nine; and high, grades ten through twelve. Located in perfect juxtaposition between these two buildings and completing the semi-circle, were three, single-story stone buildings that housed the library, the cafeteria, and the infirmary.

Beyond the stone buildings, located on the perimeter of the property were various maintenance buildings. And scattered amidst the bucolic, pine- and oak-wooded landscape were the individual bungalows where the full-time faculty lived, one of the contractual requirements that went with teaching at Wood Rose. Faculty members had to live on the orphanage property in the housing provided. All staff, however, lived off the orphanage property except for the dorm mother, Ms. Larkins, and Mrs. Ball, Headmaster Harcourt's long-time secretary. She had moved into her bungalow only a few years earlier, shortly after her husband died, with the full approval of Dr. Harcourt, the board of directors, and Miss Alcott, the major financial supporter of Wood Rose.

The number of bungalows had steadily increased over the years to where there were now fifteen bungalows in all, each constructed in white clapboard with gray slate roofs, with a comfortable interior layout that gave the on-campus faculty residents the option of cooking in their own kitchens or eating in the cafeteria. Dr. Harcourt and his wife lived in the largest bungalow, of course, which had two bedrooms. Other faculty members with spouses also lived in two-bedroom bungalows, although theirs didn't have as much square footage as the headmaster's or as much landscaping. The single faculty members and Mrs. Ball were given the smallest of the bungalows that had one bedroom. And Ms. Larkins, a single woman who had been divorced for several years, had a small private apartment in the dormitory building.

Carolina loved her little house—having her space—and the privacy and independence it afforded even if it was a bit like living in a fish bowl. After all, the distance between the dormitory and the bungalows wasn't that much. On more than one occasion since her arrival to Wood Rose she had sensed that she was being spied on, and even thought she saw binoculars poking out of a second-floor dormitory window—where the upper-class residents, ages 15 through 18, lived—aimed in her direction.

Still. She took special pride in her bungalow, lovingly and with a great deal of thought decorating each of the small rooms—Italian Provincial, and happy colors of blue and yellow with splashes of burnt orange. The bungalow had come sparsely furnished, but Carolina, using the sewing machine borrowed from Dr. Dolores Smythe, expert in international affairs, geography, and politics, in no time or effort at all had worked wonders with slip covers and cushions, a few throw rugs and, most recently, ivory damask draperies for her bedroom.

And outside, on the little plot of land where her house squatted, she added to the boxwood hedges and single camellia bush already planted those things she knew would thrive in the Piedmont soil of North Carolina: daffodil bulbs, azaleas, and forsythia bushes in anticipation of spring; hydrangeas and pyracantha with its red berries for the hot summers and autumn; two holly bushes for the winter. It was her own touch, and it gave her bungalow a slightly different appearance from the others; better attended.

Landscaping was something the previous tenant had neglected either out of laziness or because his interests took him elsewhere. She guessed the latter since she had been quietly informed by another one of her colleagues, Dr. Frank Sturdavant, professor of math, calculus, and statistics, that the man had been released from all duties a short two months after he had been hired. Apparently his lifestyle was in direct opposition to the morals and teachings Wood Rose was trying to instill in its all-female students. This last bit of information had been revealed through a twitching lip, a wrinkled forehead, and one profound snort.

Carolina owned a white Honda Civic, but she rarely drove her car unless it was to go into town to shop for incidentals like fabrics or thread for sewing, or a few groceries for those times when she needed a break from cafeteria food, or if she felt the need to explore somewhere beyond the walls, in which case she usually took the FIGs with her. In moving to Wood Rose, she found that everything both necessary and important in her life, with the exception of Larry, existed within the walls of the orphanage. Now, however, those things extended beyond those walls, and they included her mother—a traveler, a gypsy.

From her living room window, Carolina looked out into the darkness. Jimmy Bob had driven by in his old pickup truck earlier on his usual rounds, checking the insulated property and making sure all was as it should be. Stone apparitions—familiar and functional in daylight—now seemed unfamiliar and somewhat threatening in the soft illumination of the quarter moon high overhead; and everywhere dark, elongated shadows crisscrossed the lawn dampened by night-cooled air. The stillness was broken only by the rhythmic croaking of frogs from a nearby pond, an occasional splash, a mocking bird off in the distance, and the slight rustle of leaves. As she continued to gaze across the large expanse of lawn covered in glistening dew, shadowed with tall pines and massive oak trees draped in Spanish moss, she noticed three dark figures running from the building that housed the administration offices toward the dormitory. "Uh oh," she muttered under her breath. "What have they done now?"

CHAPTER THREE

*L*yuba decided not to go with the other gypsy women into the village. Instead, she would stay behind and prepare her potions from the roots she had dug in the early, pre-dawn hours in the dark of the quarter moon, always careful to replant a good piece of a root to grow next year. The day before she had picked herbs, during that time when the essential oils are at their strongest, before they could get evaporated by the midday sun. From the roots, bark and hard seeds gathered, she would make decoctions by soaking them overnight and boiling them the next day. Some of the decoctions she would add honey or sugar to; others she would thicken into syrup or add lard to make ointments and salves. She saved the freshest herbs for her oils.

The other gypsy women picked their herbs carelessly anywhere, or they would buy them dried from a shop, claiming good results. But the *Kaulo Camio*, a black gypsy who went by the name of Lyuba, knew better. She treated all plants kindly and with respect in order to capture their full spiritual healing essence. For she believed as good gypsies did that everything has a spirit, even the stones on the ground; and everything could bring good luck or bad.

She watched the gypsy women climb into the back of the pickup truck, talking and laughing, and waited until the old truck disappeared around the sharp bend in the road. They would spend the day in the nearby village selling their trinkets and wares, reading palms—"handwalking" she called it, and perhaps the Tarot cards, whatever was asked for by the settlers, or *gorgia,* and sufficiently paid for. "Settlers" were the people who lived in that area of northern Italy where they had been camping for the past few weeks. As autumn approached, however, it would soon be time for the *Kaulo Camioes*, or Black Gypsies as they were called by the settlers, to once again move south toward the warmer climes where they would spend the winter. The Bandoleer, the leader of their tribe, had not yet said if they would be stopping by the Old Villa in Frascati again. She would prepare a special *parik-til* just in case to give to Signor and Signora Granchelli for being so caring to her daughter when she was sick. Perhaps she would be lucky and once again meet with the lady at the adoption agency also, Signora Lucia De Rossa, the kind one who had tried to help her all those many years ago when her child had been taken from her. She would prepare a special *parik-til* to give to her as well because these two women shared a history and a special bond of love.

She returned to her hut and began her work. Once her potions were ready, she would take them into the village to sell. Coughs or colds, rheumatism, cuts and bruises, burns—it didn't matter. She knew what remedy was necessary to relieve pain, create lustrous hair, revive the impotent, whiten teeth, cure constipation, or simply heal the broken spirit. Unlike others who only pretended, she had the gift.

But that would be tomorrow. Today, after her work was complete, she would teach the children. Lyuba was a *choovihni*—a wise woman, something to which she was born into because of her special gift. As her birthright, she and she alone had been given the responsibility to pass on the knowledge of the travelers to the ones who would follow. Today she would teach the younger children about the roots and herbs and how to capture their full spiritual healing powers. Now that Milosh was no longer with them to constantly stir up trouble, life was easier within the camp; there was less friction among the children; the blackness had disappeared. Lyuba regretted that Milosh, the only son of the Bandoleer, had been banned from his tribe. But his *chakra*, that point of light indicating the heart, was dark and brown rather than green as it should be. Much had been expected of Milosh, but unlike his father, he was impatient and quick to judge others. His focus was on material things, and he ignored what was important. There was also a darkness in his spirit; something that proved to be dangerous, almost deadly. It was because of his transgressions that Carolina almost died, and it was also because of those transgressions that the *kris* ruled he be banned from his tribe. Milosh paid the ultimate price for his evil actions. There were no other options. That was gypsy law.

The children she would teach on this day were bright and eager, but she was yet to find a child born with the natural gift. Those children were rare. In all her years as a *choovihni*, she had only known one—the precious one that was taken from her so long ago, and who then returned to find her. Her own daughter, Carolina. Carolina didn't yet know she had the gift, and Lyuba hadn't felt it necessary to tell her. Carolina would learn of her gift when she most needed it. That was the way it was; that was the way it should be.

Lyuba carefully placed a small measure of the herbs in a bottle and covered them with olive oil. Sealing the bottle tightly with a cork, she put it with the others where they would be gently warmed by the sun. She felt the joy of contentment. The zee, the essence of all life both animate and inanimate, had chosen to smile upon her.

CHAPTER FOUR

As soon as Dara, Mackenzie, and Jennifer walked into the dining room, everything became quiet. Not even a dish rattled. The FIGs were accustomed to being talked about and made the prime subjects of gossip, and they simply chose to ignore it. They got their plates, filled them with food, and, as they always did, picked out one of the small round tables strictly reserved for faculty, apart from everyone else, where they could talk without being overheard.

Within the walls of Wood Rose, as with most closed communities, information could be sent and received through osmosis. Everyone knew everything that was happening, especially whenever there was a "situation" on campus. This morning in the cafeteria it was no different, and all of the student-residents, seated at their assigned tables in the dining room according to age and class, were discussing what had taken place during the night while they slept, and guessing what would come of it.

"Dr. Harcourt has to get rid of them and not wait until the end of summer," insisted one of the recently graduated high school seniors who had thrived in the strict environment of Wood Rose and would continue her advanced studies in religion beginning that fall at the Wake Forest School of Divinity a few miles away. "They are weird, and all they do is cause trouble." She had made this same argument many times before, the others at her table were quick to notice. They were also quick to notice that her comments seemed to be a little unforgiving.

Another girl—Lynda spelled with a "y" Corgill—who had entered Wood Rose a couple of years after Dara and Mackenzie and was now a rising junior had always secretly admired the

FIGs and didn't wish to see them get punished. Knowing that they would soon be leaving to pursue their degrees in higher education, she felt obliged, even driven, to take over where they would leave off once they were no longer on campus. In fact, while the FIGs and Carolina had been in Italy, she had taken it upon herself to try out her own creative expression by filling the lock on the headmaster's office door with an especially quick-drying cement glue in the middle of the night. It had been disappointing that even though the FIGs were thousands of miles away in Italy, they still got blamed for her expression. Nevertheless, she was undaunted. Once the FIGs were no longer on campus, she would keep practicing, with the help of one of the younger students—a squeaky-voiced kid nicknamed "Frog" who exhibited an extraordinary amount of bravery for being only 10 years old—until she was able to achieve the same vaulted status as the FIGs. Now, apparently, the FIGs had once again accomplished something quite remarkable during the middle of the night, which was why there had been so much chatter in the dining room that morning—at least until the FIGs arrived.

"But what happened?" asked one of the 11-year-old middle-grade school girls who had noticed that there were no lights on in the administration building—specifically in the headmaster's office and the office of his secretary, Mrs. Ball, which was very unusual. Another 10 year old sitting next to her had noticed as well, but didn't say anything. She was afraid of the dark and just hoped that whatever was wrong in the administration building wouldn't find its way to the cafeteria. The older girls seated nearby made spooky noises at the younger girls and giggled.

The youngest girls, ages 5 through 9, sat together at one long table in the center of the dining room. They didn't know what was going on; only that something terrible must have happened since all of the big girls were whispering. Usually, the older girls didn't whisper so much.

Separated from the long tables where the girls ate, at smaller, individual tables positioned in front of the floor-to-ceiling windows which provided scenic views of the beautifully landscaped lawn, the faculty ate in intimate groups of two, three, or four, their conversations kept to low, hushed tones.

"Of course it had to be the FIGs. How do you think they did it?" Even though the others at the table were thinking it, Dr. Rankin, head of the biology department, boldly blurted out his question first. The other three faculty members seated at the table, all teachers at the high school level, only shook their heads, not daring to make eye contact; as though afraid that if they even spoke the word FIG out loud, they would once again be saddled with trying to teach them.

At a table across the way in front of another window the conversation took on a different twist. "Maybe the FIGs didn't do it; maybe it was caused by a power surge from an alien aircraft." Clyde Benson, head of the physical education department, laughed out loud at this suggestion and then quickly sobered so as not to insult his colleague, the pretty Dr. Catherine Sullivan, head of the history and astronomy departments, whom he had been seeing with some regularity in their off hours. As usual, she once again had offered an explanation that involved aliens since she had a keen interest in panspermia, the belief that life exists throughout the universe.

"This is what I came up with last night," said Mackenzie whipping out her small computerized tablet that she carried everywhere attached to her belt. It was one of the few extravagances that had been allowed for in the strict Wood Rose budget, taking into consideration Mackenzie's high intellect. After clicking a few keys she found what she was looking for, and she held it up for Dara and Jennifer to see. It was a grid of New York City. On the grid, in addition to main points of interest, were five red dots. "Those are the addresses of the five women," she said as she took a large bite of her scrambled eggs. Dara and Jennifer leaned closer to get a better look.

"They are really scattered, aren't they—all over the city?" noted Dara. She also ate some of the scrambled eggs she had on her plate as well as a piece of bacon.

"Let me see that," said Jennifer, flipping her long blond ponytail and ignoring the two slices of toast she had on her plate. Taking the tablet, she turned it upside down, artistically drew a line connecting the four red dots forming a square, then connected the dots diagonally. The exact center of the "X" created by the diagonal lines was where the fifth dot was located. She showed it to Mackenzie and Dara. "It looks like a perfect square with an 'X' marking the fifth dot!"

The three FIGs stared at the small computer. By connecting the red dots, a perfect square was formed. And the fifth dot, in addition to marking the fifth address, seemed to be located at Grand Central Terminal. "Do you think it is some sort of code?" Mackenzie asked, her large hazel eyes wide with anticipation, the words "some sort" sounding more like "thom thort" because she was feeling a little anxious. Then as though in answer to her own question, she grabbed the tablet and immediately began inserting calculations next to each red dot, her genius stimulated.

By the end of the allotted scheduled time for breakfast, with the exception of Mackenzie who had eaten everything on her plate as well as the two slices of toast on Jennifer's plate, and the remaining piece of bacon from Dara's, the morning meal had basically been ignored at the small round table positioned off to one side in that part of the dining room reserved for faculty. The three FIGs would have a great deal to discuss with Carolina as soon as she returned to her bungalow following her meeting with Headmaster Harcourt.

***

Carolina hurried along the brick pathway, bordered by the late-summer blooms of orange and yellow marigolds that snaked between the library and infirmary toward the administration building. Up ahead she saw several other faculty members, the early-morning walkers and joggers, standing in a group whispering among themselves. They were all facing in the same direction and appeared to be staring at the building that housed the administration offices; in particular, Dr. Harcourt's and Mrs. Ball's offices. Carolina's heart quickened. The summer heat made the air heavy and muggy. Even so, Carolina felt a chill as she overheard one of her colleagues say the word "sacrilege." This was not good. She took a deep breath, trying to forget the three dark figures she had seen running across the moon-lit lawn earlier that morning. As she approached the others, someone noticed her and, like in the biblical story of Moses parting the Red Sea, everyone silently stood aside making room for her to pass.

Carolina was early for her meeting with Dr. Harcourt, even though she had taken extra time to put on make-up and dress appropriately so that Mrs. Ball wouldn't give her "that look." She had been attempting to get on Mrs. Ball's good side ever since arriving at the orphanage, but had miserably failed. "She is such a prune," Carolina had muttered into the bathroom mirror earlier that morning, as she secured her hair off her face with hair clips and applied some blush. For some reason, she just couldn't seem to get it right around that woman. Mrs. Ball had been a fixture at Wood Rose even before Dr. Harcourt had been named headmaster, having served as secretary to two previous headmasters. She knew all of its secrets, but Carolina was certain she would never reveal them. Carolina was also certain that if Mrs. Ball didn't like a member of the faculty—or staff, Dr. Harcourt didn't either, and for that reason they wouldn't be allowed to stay around for long, like the previous tenant of her bungalow.

Mrs. Ball was, after all, part of the highly-regarded, much-respected tradition of Wood Rose. A superior academic program, routine, discipline, and the much-maligned code of dress—an assortment of required clothing for outer wear, under wear, and sleep wear appropriate for recreation, classrooms, and chapel which varied only slightly according to the age of the resident—created the foundation on which Wood Rose Orphanage and Academy for Young Women had been built in the capital city of North Carolina. The founding fathers in 1894 had insisted on it, and from then until now it suited those who financially supported the orphanage and school.

The Methodist Church was one of the largest supporters with an annual contribution that more than adequately took care of 35 percent of the administrative costs. A representative from the Methodist Church sat on the Board of Directors along with eleven other members from the community—successful business leaders for the most part—whose combined donations totaled another 14 percent. This group of twelve, reverently referred to as the twelve disciples by those who lived and worked at Wood Rose, also organized an annual Christmas fund-raising charity ball from which all proceeds were donated to the orphanage for expenses not covered in the budget, such as landscape beautification or local field trips when deemed appropriate.

In addition, there were several State grants earmarked for special educational programs awarded to the orphanage each year, as well as the occasional donation from individuals who wanted to "help the poor little dears."

Finally, there was Miss Edna Grace Alcott, the feisty eighty-seven year old great niece of Horace Alcott, a tobacco farmer who had originally endowed the orphanage in the late nineteenth century. She contributed the remaining funds necessary to keep Wood Rose running successfully. In recognition of her continued philanthropy and generous spirit, the chapel had been given her family name: Alcott Chapel. A large portrait of Miss Alcott hung next to an equally large portrait of her uncle, both done in oils, in the vestibule above a Queen Ann console table. Centered on the table where it could be observed each Sunday before services—and after—was a large Waterford crystal vase filled with pink roses; something Miss Alcott had specifically requested since the pink roses complimented the pale pink color of the garment she wore in the portrait. These roses were replaced with fresh ones every Saturday morning, without fail; another request.

Dr. Thurgood James Harcourt had served as headmaster at Wood Rose for twenty-seven years. During his tenure, enrollment had remained fairly constant, ranging between thirty-eight and forty residents, as it had since the beginning except during the height of the Depression when enrollment skyrocketed to over one hundred. For the first twelve years as headmaster, he proudly maintained the proper image that was expected of an institution with affiliations to the Methodist Church and support from the pillars of the community; and even though nothing remarkable occurred during this time, nothing improper occurred either. Then the first two FIGs arrived. Adjustments had to be made; certain challenges met. The newest young residents had difficulty fitting in with the other, already-established residents; therefore, it was determined soon after their arrival that the FIGs would be happier if their rooms were located near one another in the same suite. Also, an extra floor monitor was assigned to help watch after the high-spirited girls with exceptional minds. Then there was the ongoing challenge of developing an educational program above and beyond what was offered the other students their same age in order to meet their intellectual needs. Often this extra work created discontent among the faculty along with feelings of inadequacy.

Negative press, which had never been a problem prior to the girls' arrival, now seemed to be a constant threat. This could result in smaller donations which would mean the difference between either meeting budget needs or having to reduce the already limited number of faculty positions. When the third FIG arrived only a short time before Carolina assumed her new post, other adjustments had to be made and different challenges met causing Dr. Harcourt to question whether it was worth having three intellectually superior residents who were full of *joie de vivre* if they were going to cause so much unneeded upheaval and distraction—as well as the uninvited interest among members of the local, regional, and potentially national news media. All of the effort he had expended over the years to maintain a positive, dignified image of Wood Rose with the press and the community at large now occasionally took on a carnival atmosphere.

However, at age fifty-nine, slightly stooped, with gray thinning hair, but otherwise healthy and with no desire to retire early, he had managed to keep the reputation of Wood Rose unsullied, and he did so with firmness and decorum. No one was more dedicated or intimately involved in the detailed operations of the orphanage than Dr. Harcourt; and no one took greater interest in its success. The dark gray suites he wore, the conservative gray-striped ties which might give way to a smidgeon of maroon on special celebratory occasions, and his stern demeanor were a reflection of the rules of strict discipline and unwavering routine that had been passed down to him from previous headmasters; and it suited his nature.

As Carolina entered through the hallowed front doors of the sanctified administration building, she wondered why it was so dark. The double wooden doors leading to Mrs. Ball's office as well as Dr. Harcourt's beyond were standing wide open, and Carolina was surprised to see the headmaster's diminutive secretary crawling around on the floor, looking under furniture.

"Mrs. Ball? Can I help you find something?" Then glancing around, "Why is it so dark in here?"

Mrs. Ball stood up then, brushed off her dress that was dark blue, for she felt it was her duty to adhere to the same strict dress code—at least in color—as the student/residents at Wood Rose, and squared back her shoulders. "That look" then followed as she put Carolina's pink blush, pink lipstick, brushed hair, skirt and blouse, and sandals under full scrutiny. "Somehow, some way, all of the light bulbs in all of the light fixtures in the entry foyer, in my office, and in Dr. Harcourt's office have disappeared," she said, motioning expansively with one hand. "Just mysteriously vanished," she said, this time with more emphasis and extending both of her arms to include everything as far as the eye could see and not see.

"My goodness, how on earth did that happen?" But Carolina didn't have to ask.

Just then Dr. Harcourt came out of his office following the illumination of a large flashlight. "This really is deplorable..." then he saw Carolina. Stopping in mid-sentence, he motioned with his flashlight and led her back into his dark office where the only light visible was the natural light filtering through the large window which afforded him full view of his prize *Photinia frasen,* the beautifully landscaped campus of Wood Rose, and the ivy-covered stone walls beyond. Carolina's attempt at a confident smile fell a little short, as it usually did whenever she entered the headmaster's office that smelled heavily of wood wax and lavender, Mrs. Ball's favorite scent. She heard Mrs. Ball close the door firmly behind her.

Mahogany-paneled, thickly-carpeted, and enveloped in dark green fabric, the headmaster's office always made Carolina feel like she should whisper, or maybe bow her head. She wasn't even Catholic, yet once again she felt the overpowering need to cross herself and kiss her thumb as she had seen others of the Catholic faith do. Perhaps even genuflect.

He didn't waste any time on small talk. "Well, Ms. Lovel, it appears *your* three students have done it again." His emphasis on the word "your" did not go unnoticed by Carolina. He sighed deeply and flopped down into his desk chair, only to immediately jump up again when the crunching sound of broken glass filled the darkened room. "Mrs. Ball," he yelled, "I found the light bulbs. Get hold of Jimmy Bob before he leaves and tell him to bring us a new supply."

If her mission hadn't been so important, Carolina would have laughed openly. Instead, she bit her bottom lip and immediately started picking up the larger pieces of broken light bulbs that had fallen to the floor, arranging them in a neat pile on the headmaster's desk. Jimmy Bob would have to use the vacuum to get the smaller pieces. She only hoped none of the glass shards had torn Dr. Harcourt's trousers. She bit her bottom lip harder and remained standing.

"So what urgent matter brings you here this morning," he asked, moving away from the mess in his black leather chair. After illuminating it with the flash light to make sure there weren't any more hidden light bulbs, he then sat down on the dark green sofa placed near the multi-paned window flanked by dark green draperies from where he could keep a watchful eye on his prize *Photinia frasen.* There had been a nice, heavy dew during the night, and with the extra warm day-time temperatures, his bush was thriving in spite of the brutal whacking the FIGs had given it before going to Italy.

Carolina decided to get right to the point. The FIGs had written up their findings regarding the Voynich Manuscript and presented them to the head of special research projects at the Beinecke Library with a copy to Dr. Harcourt the day after they returned from Italy. That would be as good a place to start as any. "I know how busy you are, Dr. Harcourt"—it never hurt to try to soften his mood a bit—"but have you had a chance to read the report Dara, Mackenzie, and Jennifer prepared regarding the Voynich Manuscript?"

He thought that might be the purpose of her visit. He had read it, in fact, and was quite pleased. In fact, so much so he was seriously considering sending it as an attachment with the application for additional State funding he was preparing. "Yes, I have." He stood up and glanced out the window, as though expecting to see the FIGs there hacking away at his bush. "I must admit, I am very impressed." Satisfied that his bush was safe for the time being, he sat back down. "In fact, I am thinking of including it with the grant application I am preparing."

This was going much better than Carolina had expected. "As you know, the Voynich Manuscript is now being kept at the Beinecke Library at Yale University. I have been communicating with Dr. Pedigrew, the head of special research projects, and he has invited us—the girls and me—to meet with him to discuss our findings."

"Ms. Lovel, budget…"

Carolina quickly interrupted, "Dr. Pedigrew mentioned wanting to publish the report in their journal. Of course, any recognition the girls were to receive would directly reflect on Wood Rose Orphanage and Academy for Young Women and would probably help with securing the grant—maybe even increase the amount of funding."

The headmaster didn't say anything, his eyes behind his dark-framed glasses thoughtful. Carolina continued, not wanting to stop her momentum.

"And since Jennifer will be starting rehearsals for her performance at Carnegie Hall, I thought we—Dara, Mackenzie, and I—could go to New York over the summer to be with her. We could plan to meet with Dr. Pedigrew before returning to Wood Rose, just before it is time for orientation at the universities where they will be attending in late August. And just before the girls leave Wood Rose—permanently." She didn't mention paying for the trip herself. She had already paid for them to go to Italy out of the account that had been set up by her parents in her name when she was born. She would wait to see if Dr. Harcourt would offer first; if not, she could use her own money as a last resort.

Carolina could tell he was wavering. The idea of not having to deal with the FIGs' acts of creative expression for the next several weeks was very compelling. She decided to give the finance issue a little nudge. "Of course, since this is school related, and Wood Rose stands a very good chance of benefiting directly from our meeting with the head of special research projects at Beineke, not to mention Jennifer performing at Carnegie Hall over Thanksgiving and the wonderful, positive stories in the news that will create, it is appropriate that Wood Rose fund this trip." Then in a final push, she added, "If the girls aren't allowed to go, then I am afraid they will become restless no matter what projects I assign them to do." She then frowned and stared deliberately and purposefully out the window toward his bush. She would have pursed her lips as well, but she was still thinking about Harcourt sitting on all those light bulbs, and if she tried pursing her lips she might laugh.

The office became very still. Once again Dr. Harcourt stood up and looked out his window, as though reassuring himself that no harm had come to his bush in the past few minutes. The difficulty was that an off-campus trip of this nature involving

42

Wood Rose student/residents required the Board of Directors' full approval as well as Miss Alcott's. That could take days, maybe even weeks—especially if any of the Board members were on vacation. However, he reasoned, the FIGs had already graduated, and, therefore, really weren't students at Wood Rose any longer, only residents until the end of the summer when they would leave to go to the universities where they had been accepted. In fact, other than being required to wear their uniforms, for which he allowed no flexibility, and follow all of the other rules expected of the student/residents as long as they were on campus, the traveling off campus rule probably didn't even apply to them. Therefore, maybe he could get around even mentioning anything to the Board or to Miss Alcott who had a tendency to be somewhat sharp-tongued and opinionated.

As he continued looking out the window he saw the FIGs, dressed in their school uniforms, run out of the cafeteria toward the bungalow where Ms. Lovel lived. Except for the white cotton undergarments which were bought from the discount store in bulk to fit all sizes, the clothing provided at Wood Rose was either dark blue or pale yellow. The school class uniforms worn by the girls in high school consisted of a pale yellow blouse that was worn with a dark blue skirt, unlike the yellow blouses and blue jumpers worn by the elementary and middle-grade girls. All of the Wood Rose girls were required to wear dark blue socks and black, lace-up shoes until they reached high school. At that time they could do away with the dark blue socks and black lace-up shoes and either wear blue tights with black pumps or, in the hot summer months of July and August, black pumps without tights. The class uniforms were also worn to Sunday services.

In addition to the class uniforms, the residents at Wood Rose were supplied shorts, t-shirts, and tennis shoes for gym class and recreational activities, coats and gloves for cold weather, rain gear for inclement weather—all dark blue and pale yellow—and, of course, the white under garments. By providing uniforms for the residents, feelings of jealousy over clothing were eliminated, it was believed by Dr. Harcourt and the members of the Board, and the girls' focus could be turned to more important, productive things, such as academics.

In spite of the inflexibility of rules regarding the dress code, the FIGs, however, had found how to demonstrate their individuality and qualities of genius by the subtle ways in which they wore their uniforms. Dara, the tallest and also the most outgoing of the three FIGs, always wore her pale yellow blouse with the first two buttons open, thus revealing more of her skin than was necessary in the opinion of the faculty, staff, and administration. Mackenzie, on the other hand, a little on the heavy side, who had a tendency to lisp whenever she got nervous, wore her blouse with all of the buttons closed. And Jennifer, petite and blond, who occasionally displayed outbursts of uncontrollable anger, chose to express her individuality in a different way altogether that didn't even involve the blouse. She didn't wear any underwear. Of course, this wasn't as obvious as the buttoned or unbuttoned blouses, but she knew she didn't have any underwear on, and so did the other FIGs.

The three uniforms, and the girls wearing them, having once reached Carolina's bungalow, plopped down on the front steps to wait for her to return from her meeting with the headmaster. Dara sat on the top step, both feet firmly planted in front of her, knees together, looking straight ahead. Mackenzie sat next to Dara, pulling at her skirt as she crossed her legs. And Jennifer, flipping her long, blond ponytail and turning at an angle toward Mackenzie and Dara, sat on the step just below them. Mackenzie fluffed her short brown hair and giggled, Jennifer rocked back and forth to the musical beat only she could hear, while Dara simply continued to stare stoically straight ahead.

It was the expressions of individuality in which the FIGs wore the uniforms, however, that the headmaster now focused his critical attention on as he stood at his window. Having read many books on character development and personality disorders, and considering himself an expert in most matters involving the human psyche, Dr. Harcourt naturally noticed the unbuttoned blouse worn by Dara. She was, after all, narcissistic—believing that the world revolved around her—in his educated opinion. The buttoned blouse worn by Mackenzie, an obvious display of anxiety paralysis, only confirmed his belief that she suffered from the condition of paranoia. He wondered what he was missing when he glanced at Jennifer—she was probably a borderline personality with a tendency toward violence. In any case, he decided that along with the traveling off campus rule, their slight dress code indiscretions weren't worth mentioning to the Board either. Or to Miss Alcott.

At the same moment he reached that conclusion, there was a light tap on his office door. "Jimmy Bob is here with the light bulbs," Mrs. Ball informed her boss. "If there aren't enough, he said he could go into town to get more."

"When would you leave?" he asked Carolina.

"As soon as possible."

"Do it!"

CHAPTER FIVE

*L*yuba filled her basket with the things she had prepared the day before: small bags of dried herbs, jars of ointment, and pretty bottles of oil. She also wrapped her crystal in the soft, black cloth and tucked it in at one end along with her Tarot cards which she protected in a box covered with a scarf of black silk. She preferred to read palms—handwalking, she called it—but if someone asked for the crystal or cards, she would be prepared. The last thing she added was a *parik-til* she had made, just in case there was a need.

The Bandoleer had told her earlier that morning that they would be breaking camp soon in order to take advantage of the nice weather to travel. He also told her that he had decided they would once again stop in Frascati for several days before journeying farther south. Even though it held bad memories for him, for that was where Milosh, his son, had been banned from the tribe, the area had always provided them a rich source of income. And the area where they set up camp in the shadows of the Old Villa was safe.

That had made Lyuba happy, for it was there that Carolina, her daughter, again found her after having been taken from her by that heartless *gorgia* so long ago. It had been a beautiful spring day, much like this one, when Lyuba decided to take her young daughter with her into the village. She was such a pretty, happy little girl—fair complexioned, large green eyes, and beautiful dark hair. Nothing like her parents who were dark skinned and showed all of the physical characteristics of the black tribe. It happened—a white child born into the black tribe—but only rarely. How proud Lyuba was of Carolina, a special child who had been born with the gift. Normally, Lyuba would leave her daughter behind at the camp where she would be protected. She wasn't yet old enough to understand the ways of the settlers and how to deal with them. But it was such a nice day. The little girl, not yet four years old, would draw attention. People would buy Lyuba's potions when they saw Carolina.

But that's not what happened. Lyuba knew as soon as she got to the village that she had made a mistake in bringing her child. Evil was lurking nearby; all of the omens were present. She fled, taking the back streets out of town and then cutting through the gardens of the Old Villa. But the rushed pace tired her child, and carrying her slowed Lyuba. Instead of getting her daughter to safety, Carolina was taken by a man with the government agency. For weeks Lyuba begged him to give her back; after all, she was recently widowed, and Carolina was all she had left. In desperation, she even broke into the building where Carolina was being kept in an attempt to find her only child. They could have had her arrested, but they did not. Nor would they relent. And then Lyuba knew. Because her powers were innate, bred through a bloodline of generations of psychics, she knew that Carolina was no longer there. They had given her away to other parents in another country.

Heartbroken, Lyuba did something she had never done before: She put a curse on the man who was responsible for her pain. She wanted to make him suffer as he had made her suffer. A short time later, the travelers broke camp and continued on their journey, never to return until just recently—when her beautiful daughter—now a grown woman—found her in the place where she had been taken from all those years ago.

Smiling, and with her basket in tow, Lyuba glanced toward the shadow of the tall elm tree. It was getting on toward mid-morning—time for the villagers to be up and about. Most of the gypsy women had left earlier, preferring to ride in the back of the pickup truck. As usual, she preferred to walk. Two other women, also walking into the village, hurried to join her.

"So, Lyuba, do you think we will have a good day?" The young woman who asked the question was eager, but untrained. She had much to learn of the ways of the settlers she wished to sell to. If she presented herself in an aggressive manner, they would turn away from her. Lyuba nodded but didn't speak. The other woman sensed Lyuba's mood and pulled the young woman back. It was better to leave Lyuba alone with her thoughts.

CHAPTER SIX

*W*alking from the darkness of the administration building into the brilliant early-morning sunlight Carolina could hardly contain her happiness—for Dara, but also for Mackenzie and Jennifer as well. And for herself. She had been trying to come up with something exciting for them to do over the summer, but after their adventures in Italy, everything she thought of fell short and flat, inadequate and uninteresting. Now, they had a plan.

Reaching into the pocket of her skirt, she pulled out her cell phone and quick-dialed Larry's number. Summer classes had already started at the University of North Carolina where he taught psychology, but all of his classes were scheduled in the afternoon. He answered on the second ring. "I was just thinking about you."

"You are such a charmer," Carolina said, the love she felt for this man who was the son of a Gypsy King spilling out into her words and her smile, then she gave him a quick update on her meeting with Dr. Harcourt which included the light bulbs.

"You mean he sat on them?"

"I'm afraid so. I was terrified he might have a piece of glass stuck in his... well... you know... trousers, but I didn't dare offer to look."

"When are you planning to leave?"

"Just as soon as we can. I really don't want to waste any time."

"I can help," offered Larry. "There is a 9 o'clock direct flight leaving from Raleigh-Durham into LaGuardia. If it isn't already sold out, I'll get you tickets for tomorrow. I'll plan on taking you to the airport—say around 7 tomorrow morning. That will give us plenty of time to get all of you checked in." Then, reality setting in, less enthusiastically, "That means you will be gone all summer. I'll miss you, Carolina."

"I'll miss you, too, Larry." Then after a pause, "I have to go with them, you know."

"Yeah, I know."

"Maybe you can come to New York between summer school sessions."

"Maybe." His mind was racing. "Do you know where you'll want to stay?" He knew she probably hadn't even thought about it.

"No, not yet. But I'm sure we can find something once we get there."

"Listen, I know someone—a guy—his name is Grai. He will take you wherever you need to go while you are in New York. Also, there is a boarding house where you can stay until you are ready to come back. Mrs. Killebrew who runs it is a little bit crusty, but her bark is worse than her bite. It isn't anything fancy, but it is clean and the food is good. I think you and the FIGs will like it."

"Larry, you are wonderful. You really are."

"Yeah, I know. Look, I have a student coming in now so I have to go. I'll see you in the morning."

Carolina slipped the phone back into her pocket. Larry was being so understanding, especially since they had only just gotten back from Italy and the two of them hadn't been able to spend much time together. But this was something she had to do. Dara, Mackenzie, and Jennifer had been there for her when she needed them. Now, she needed to be there for them. After all, they were her responsibility, but even more than that, she felt like she was one of them.

Ms. Larkins, busy washing and drying bed sheets for the dorm residents, had spotted Carolina going into the dark administration building earlier and was watching for her to come back out. She had overheard rumblings of something that the FIGs had done overnight. No one was quite sure what it was though other than it had something to do with the headmaster's administration offices. With an armload of warm sheets just taken from the dryer, she positioned herself outside the dormitory entrance where she had full view of the administration building. Within a few short minutes, Carolina appeared.

Ignoring the walkway, Ms. Larkins ran across the lawn carrying the clean dry sheets. "Yoohoo!" She was determined to do or say whatever was necessary to avoid being sucked into the blame for whatever the FIGs had done this time. She alone was responsible for the girls' safe keeping between the hours of 10 o'clock in the evening and 7 o'clock in the morning. Other than severe illness or some natural disaster like a hurricane, there was no excuse for any of the girls to be out of bed, and certainly not out of their rooms, during those hours. After that offense when the FIGs had "foiled" Dr. Harcourt's office, Ms. Larkins had taken added precautions to insure that she would be awakened if anyone were to attempt to leave the dormitory in the middle of the night. A string tied from the outer door to a bell she had next to her bed, and it should have worked. It didn't. And the additional string she tied from the window on the second floor to the same little bell also didn't work when the FIGs pruned the headmaster's bush. And now this—whatever "this" was. "Is everything all right?" she asked Carolina, slightly out of breath.

"Everything is fine, Ms. Larkins, why do you ask?"

Ms. Larkins glanced toward the headmaster's large window that overlooked his prize bush and just then saw light suddenly stream from it. Feeling a little bit better, she saw other windows near the headmaster's light up one by one. "Well, it is a beautiful day, isn't it?" No need to get defensive and make excuses for herself if there wasn't any reason to.

"Yes, it is," said Carolina brightly. "You have a nice day."

Up ahead, Carolina noticed the three FIGs sitting on the front steps of her bungalow. As soon as they saw her, they ran to meet her, and immediately all four women started talking at once. Two bungalows down from Carolina's, Dr. Elizabeth

Humphry, professor of English literature, Romance languages, and art history, opened her front door and stepped out onto her small front porch to see what all of the commotion was about. Elizabeth's eyes widened to the extent that they emerged above the round, black-framed glasses she wore to correct a bad case of stigmatism and near-sightedness as she heard the words "New York," "glass," "non-stop," "Mr. Grai," "light bulbs," "Larry," "boarding house," "Grand Central Terminal," and "square." Shaking her head in utter disdain and fearful disbelief, she hurried back into the safe environment of her bungalow, closing and locking the door with exaggerated determination.

She knew there had been some sort of problem with the electricity in the administration building that morning. Dr. Dolores Smythe, expert in international affairs, geography, and politics, and Dr. George Connoly, professor of physics and chemistry, had told her that earlier at breakfast. Dolores felt it was probably just a blown fuse, but George gave a more detailed explanation, one that neither of the women understood, involving transformers, high voltage, and short circuits. Whatever it was, Dr. Smythe had no doubt that the FIGs were behind it. A couple of months earlier, they had wrapped Dr. Harcourt's pristine office in aluminum foil. Everything—pens, sheets of paper, curtains, desk, rugs, telephone, computer—was covered in silver. Even the paperclips piled in the black-veined onyx bowl, a gift from another graduating class, were each individually wrapped. Nothing had escaped.

Punishment had been light, too light in Dr. Smythe's opinion, considering it was their latest "creative expression" as it was referred to around campus in a long line of inappropriate, disruptive behavior they had subjected Dr. Harcourt to over the years, probably because he realized they would be graduating soon, leaving Wood Rose, and he wouldn't have to be concerned with them any longer. They were ordered to unwrap everything and then were confined to their dorm rooms for two weeks other than going to the cafeteria for meals, or the chapel for Sunday services, which was pretty much their usual routine anyway.

The month before that, it had been the discovery of unauthorized reading material—or, more explicitly, magazines revealing male nudes—in the FIGs' rooms. Contraband of this nature was totally unacceptable, stringently opposed to the morals and teachings at Wood Rose, and an extreme violation of the rules. For that, they had been assigned kitchen duty for two weeks—washing dishes and cleaning up the dining room after each meal. The symbolism in this punishment had not gone unnoticed by all who paid attention to these things.

And, of course, there had been the bush; more precisely, Dr. Harcourt's prize *Photinia frasen.*

There had been many other expressions of creativity over the years at the place where the FIGs called home, deeds that had been dutifully recorded in the historical archives at Wood Rose; but lately these expressions seemed to have taken on what most of the faculty and staff considered a more menacing tone of a sexual nature.

So whatever this was, it must really be a biggie. Dr. Smythe peeped through her curtains and watched the three FIGs and Carolina disappear into her bungalow, all four still chattering away. It was too early for lunch; she had only just finished breakfast. But she would be sure to get to the cafeteria early that day for the noon meal so as not to miss out on any of the latest news.

CHAPTER SEVEN

O nce again Dara stared into the darkness unable to sleep. She had gotten up several times to recheck her suitcase, making sure she hadn't forgotten anything. Carolina had said to pack just one bag, and the clothes she had bought to wear in Italy would be perfect. They could keep things washed up because the boarding house where they would be staying had a washer and dryer. She had felt hesitant in asking Larry if he could help find out where her mother might be. She wasn't even sure she wanted to know. But now she was glad she had asked for his help. No matter what, knowing something was better than not knowing anything.

She couldn't stop thinking about the addresses of the five women, and how when plotted on Mackenzie's grid of New York City with a line connecting them, it formed a square with the fifth dot located in the center pointing to Grand Central Terminal. What could it mean? Or was it just some strange coincidence? When they showed Carolina, she was as perplexed as they were. She had tried calling Larry to see if he had any ideas, but he didn't answer. She said he was probably in class. They would ask him on the way to the airport.

It had been ten years. Ten years of living in an orphanage. Ten years since she last saw her mother. At the time, Social Services told her she had seven older brothers and sisters, but Dara never knew them. They had already left home by the time she was born. Now, in the darkness of her room, she tried to stir what few memories she had—always feeling hungry and the pungent odor of swamp mud. They had a small garden, she remembered, but nothing much ever came of it, and there was an old, smoke-blackened pot sitting out front in the yard that her mother burned kerosene in to keep the snakes away. Her mother had told her to always run if she saw a snake, which probably explained why she had such a fear of them now. Home was a rusted-out trailer set back in a thicket near a ditch bank that usually flooded whenever it rained. Dara no longer remembered what the inside of the trailer looked like. She only remembered the two of them—her and her mother—sitting on the outside stoop listening to tree frogs and cicadas while muddy flood waters lapped at their feet. That and her mother's beautiful, red painted mouth.

She never knew her father, probably because her mother didn't know who her father was. She knew other men, though. Her mother had many male friends, all who would show up late at night dressed in their nice starched uniforms. They had come over from the US Naval base just across the ditch bank, protected by a chain-link fence in order to keep anyone out who didn't belong.

Most of the men wouldn't talk to her. But if they did, she would ask them to teach her new words. After all, they had traveled to foreign places, and Dara knew just enough to understand that people in other places spoke different languages. Sometimes the words they taught her weren't nice words, and they would laugh at her when she repeated them. Or sometimes they were made-up words just to get her out of the way. But it didn't matter. She played her game with the words, thinking about the heavy parts of the biggest words, giving them a number or weight, and figuring out where they came from and their meaning.

Neighbors who didn't have much more than Dara and her mother would occasionally give them food or maybe some clothes—hand-me-downs that their own kids had outgrown. And sometimes when one of the men left a little extra money, Dara's mother would take her into town to buy some candy at the store. That's what happened the last time Dara saw her mother. "You wait here, pretty girl," her mother had told her, poking her finger into one of the sausage curls on Dara's head to smooth it out. Dara waited hours for her mother to come back for her. But she never did.

When Social Services stepped in, Dara was given clean clothes to wear and food to eat. She was also given a battery of tests—psychological and educational performance evaluation tests they were called—to see where she should be placed in school. Astonishingly, she ranked off the charts. Thinking it was a scoring error, the child psychologist administering the tests gave them to Dara again, along with several different tests. This time Dara scored even higher, especially in the area of verbal skills—word recognition, association, and assimilation. Dr. Doris James, head of Social Services for the State of Virginia, was consulted. And it was she who decided to send Dara to Wood Rose Orphanage and Academy for Young Women. Dr. Harcourt was a long-time friend, and she knew of the sterling reputation he had maintained at Wood Rose over the years that he had been there as headmaster. She felt confident that Dara Roux, a gifted child with an obvious proclivity toward foreign languages, would be given the attention and encouragement she needed. In return, the State of Virginia would pay Wood Rose for taking care of her.

In some ways, it didn't seem as long as it had been. Mackenzie had been admitted to Wood Rose just a short time after Dara, so they had each other. Then Jennifer came a few years later. Now there was Carolina. Dara sighed, smoothed a wrinkle from the dark blue sheet covering her, trying to will herself to sleep. Mackenzie had told her she was working on a plan, something about the numbers in the addresses and east, west streets and north, south avenues.

She wondered if there were snakes in New York City.

Anyone can vanish. Maybe it is because they get lost, or maybe they get abducted, or maybe killed. Or maybe they just want to leave the place where they are and the people they know and not ever be found again.

"You wait here, pretty girl."

Finally, Dara slept.

***

Even though she hadn't finished packing, and it was already past curfew, Mackenzie continued scribbling down equations and punching in numerical codes into her small hand-held tablet beneath her dark blue bed covers. Since the rule at Wood Rose was "lights out" at 10 o'clock—even on weekends, she was using the flashlight that she always kept under her pillow in her bed. The grid she had prepared with the addresses created an unusual geometrical puzzle, and it was more than just a coincidence. No matter what equations she used, the number "61" kept coming up. Working with the numbers and the formulae that were presented, she created an algorithm from numerical codes determined to discover its meaning. After all, that was her specialty; that was what made her a genius.

Using a basic knowledge of how New York City was laid out, she knew that streets ran east-west, and avenues ran north-south. To calculate the distances in New York City, she also knew that twenty avenues and ten streets equaled one mile. But that didn't apply to parts of Greenwich Village or the lower part of Manhattan, and she allowed for that. Also, there were five boroughs—Manhattan, Brooklyn, Queens, the Bronx, and Staten Island. Based on her calculations, and looking at the relationship between the numbers of the addresses and the streets or avenues of where they were located, there was an address in each one of the five boroughs. However, the square that was created when drawing a line to connect each location and the "X" that was formed when diagonal lines were drawn connecting each corner of the square appeared to indicate a separate borough—a sixth borough.

It was getting late. Mackenzie saved her calculations so she could show them to Dara and Jennifer and Carolina the next day and then got out of bed to finish packing. Stumbling around in the dark with only the flashlight to guide her, shoving first one thing and then another into her suitcase, she couldn't stop thinking about that sixth borough. If her calculations were correct, and she knew they were, it was located at or near Grand Central Station, the place where the fifth address was as well.

At last satisfied that she had packed everything she could possibly need, she shoved the flashlight back under her pillow and crawled into bed, pulling the dark blue covers up around her neck, and poking out one foot like a barometer. Within minutes she was asleep.

***

Jennifer had packed earlier in the day, right after returning to the dorm from Carolina's bungalow. Her suitcase was now parked next to the door along with her shoulder bag where she carried her artist pad and the portfolio of blank, eight-stave paper. She had received a letter from Andrew Whatley, Director of Special Events at Carnegie Hall, which listed the days and times when the orchestra would be rehearsing her symphonic concerto in four movements, *The Gypsy Cadence*. Mr. Whatley had been there when she performed her piano sonata at the age of thirteen as well. He was looking forward to seeing her again, the letter stated, and the members of the orchestra considered it an honor to perform her beautiful and most creative symphony. She had tucked the letter into one of the side pockets of her suitcase. She was excited about the rehearsals and the actual performance of *The Gypsy Cadence*. Her music was the one single expression of herself that she could share, for it was at that moment—when she performed—that she could truly be herself. There was no accident, no orphanage, no black and white image or rock. There was only her music. Complete and fulfilling. She would think about that later, however. For now, she had other things on her mind.

Mackenzie had been banging around in her bedroom, probably because she hadn't finished packing. Ever since breakfast that morning she had been working on her computer, punching in figures and formulae. Dara had been more quiet than usual, but that was understandable. She hadn't seen her mother since she was seven years old, and now there was a possibility that she might find her.

Jennifer punched her pillow into a ball, then eased down between the dark blue sheets and summer blanket. The rock was there. And earlier, when she had finished packing, an image—black and white like a charcoal drawing—appeared. She couldn't make it out yet; it was too blurred. But she knew in time it would become clear, just before it changed to color. Then she would hear the cadence. It was starting again.

***

Jimmy Bob slowly made the rounds in his old beat-up truck, starting with the outer perimeter along the ivy-covered stone walls surrounding the Wood Rose campus, and then gradually circling his way toward the middle of the large, wooded property until finally reaching the center where the administration building was located. Without fail, the entire process took him two hours and forty-three minutes. However, on those nights when his favorite team was playing live on television—it didn't matter which sport—he would only patrol around the dormitory and the administration building, which would take fifteen minutes.

Jimmy Bob didn't like change. Born and reared in that region of North Carolina known as the Piedmont, and the only sibling out of eleven who made it to the eighth grade, he never felt any desire to visit anywhere else, much less move to. He still lived in the house where he had been brought up, at least during the day, and now alone except for old Tick, his hound dog. And the Wood Rose Orphanage and Academy for Young Women, his place of employment for the past thirty years, was only a couple of miles down the road, which is where he spent all of his nights and part of his days.

Since Jimmy Bob didn't like change, and there had never been any reason to alter this routine anyway, the time he would leave his office to go on patrol was always the same: 12 midnight. On this night, even though the favored Durham Bulls had gone into extra innings against the Indianapolis Indians, the minor league baseball game was being televised by the local station in a delayed broadcast, therefore eliminating the need for Jimmy to cut his patrol short. At exactly two hours and forty-three minutes after he started his rounds, he parked his truck and entered through the locked door of the administration building located on the east end. Within minutes he was comfortably reinstalled in his over-sized recliner positioned in front of the 12-inch television he kept in his small office. It was the top of the fifteenth inning; the Bulls 6, the Indians 5. The Indians were up to bat. Next to the recliner on a small table was a bag of cheese chips, a canned soft drink, and the pad of paper and pen he kept handy just in case he felt inspired to write something—a word, a phrase, a nice couplet. For Jimmy Bob considered himself a poet, and it was during his solitary nocturnal hours that he was able to transfer his inner-most thoughts onto paper, stringing words together into rhyming alliteration, repeating the same consonants or sounds. It was while others slept that he was his most creative; when he visualized himself as heroic, charged with the weighty responsibility of keeping all safe during those hours he referred to in meter and rhyme as "witches' moments"—the magical time that occurs between late darkness and early light.

***

The gypsy camp was full of noise and activity. Temporary outbuildings, lean-tos, and sheds were being dismantled; personal belongings were being packed and placed in wagons. A severe weather front was forecasted to be heading into the area, bringing with it heavy winds and rain for the next several days. The settlers would stay in their homes and not come out to buy from the travelers in inclement weather. So the Bandoleer had instructed the tribe to break camp sooner than they had originally planned. They would leave before daybreak the next morning. Assuming they could stay ahead of the front, and allowing for mishaps such as broken wagon wheels and lame horses, they should be able to travel 30 or 35 miles a day. It would take them four days to get to Frascati and the place in the shadows of the Old Villa next to the river where they would make their camp.

Intent on packing her belongings—she had already packed her herbs and medicinals—Lyuba was startled when she noticed the single black magpie sitting in the tall elm next to her hut. A bad omen. She reached into the fold of her skirt and felt the small stone worn smooth by the river. It had a tiny, natural hole in it; it was her lucky charm. It comforted her. For now she would finish what she must do to prepare for the journey. Later she would study the Tarot and learn of the warning the magpie had brought to her.

CHAPTER EIGHT

$\mathcal{L}$ arry had been a little surprised when Dara asked him if he could help her find her mother. But he understood. And getting a copy of her mother's birth certificate which showed her real name made it fairly easy to track where she had been these past ten years. The trail ended, however, in New York City, and that is when he contacted a boyhood friend from his tribe—also a gypsy who had decided to pursue a life outside of the gypsy culture. Since he lived and worked in New York, Larry hoped he might be able to get some additional information Dara could use in her search. He hadn't disappointed. He was able to come up with five addresses. This was the friend Larry also entrusted to keep an eye on Carolina and the FIGs while they were in New York.

Jimmy Bob Doake was standing in front of the large, black wrought iron gates leading into Wood Rose Orphanage and Academy for Young Women when Larry drove up. He had heard that Ms. Lovel was taking those three young women she taught to New York City now, even though they had only just gotten back from Italy. Her friend, Larry, was going to pick them up and take them to the airport.

Unlike some of the other faculty and staff who were jealous or could only see fault, Jimmy Bob liked Ms. Lovel. She always spoke to him and even encouraged him in his writing. The little book she had given him on how to write poetry had been very helpful for that was when he learned that not all poetry had to rhyme; that there was something called "free verse." On this particular early morning he wanted to be sure he was standing in front of the massive wrought-iron gates when Larry got there so he could let him through without any delay. Jimmy Bob might not like change, but if Ms. Lovel liked change, then he wanted to be there to help her if she needed it.

"How are you this morning, Jimmy Bob?" Larry asked. Larry had become a frequent visitor to Wood Rose since Carolina started working there, and the two men shared a common interest in baseball. "Did you see that Bulls-Indians game last night?"

"Sure did," he answered with a big grin. "It were a good one, won't it?"

Larry laughed and nodded as Jimmy Bob quickly opened the gates for him to drive through. It was a little before 7, but he imagined Carolina and the FIGs would be ready. They were. When he got to Carolina's bungalow, the four young women were waiting outside with their suitcases, shoulder bags, and an assortment of other carry-ons. Larry's car wasn't that big, and the trunk was especially small, but after a few failed attempts, and Mackenzie's calculations using a complex formula that included ratios, weights, and dimensions, and with the sheer brute strength of Jimmy Bob who had hurried over from the main gate to do what he could to help, all the luggage was secured in the trunk with Carolina and the FIGs comfortably seated in the front and back seats of the car. Within minutes, they were on their way.

"Mackenzie has something to show you," said Carolina holding up the small tablet that Mackenzie handed her. "The red dots indicate the addresses of the five women on the list you gave to Dara." She held it up so Larry could see it and still keep his eye on the road. "Now, look what Jennifer discovered." She turned it upside down so that it revealed four dots connected and forming a square. The fifth dot was in the middle. "When you draw a line diagonally from each dot, the center is exactly where the fifth dot is positioned, and guess what else is there? Grand Central Station." Larry slowed down, taking a closer look. Then he pulled off on the side of the road.

"Let me see that." He took the tablet, holding it first one way, then the other.

"The other strange thing," added Mackenzie, "is that no matter what computations I use, the number "61" keeps popping up." Keeping his eyes on the tablet, he said, "It is probably just one of those strange coincidences." He glanced at the FIGs sitting in the backseat. "Nothing to worry about," he added. But the alarms had started to go off in his mind, and because he was the son of a Gypsy King, he knew there were no coincidences in life. The four dots that created an "X" marking the fifth dot had a meaning, as did the number "61," and his instincts were telling him that it wasn't good.

By the time they got checked in at the airport, it was obvious Larry's mood had changed. The excitement and enthusiasm he had exhibited earlier when they loaded the luggage into his car had turned downright glum. And when it was time for Carolina and the FIGs to board their plane, he seemed almost despondent. He hugged each of the FIGs, and when he got to Dara, he said, "You don't have to do this, you know."

"Yes... I do," Dara answered.

Larry nodded. The cosmic events had been set in motion. There was nothing he could say or do to stop them. "I hope that what you find will give you peace."

As the three FIGs went through the boarding gate, he pulled Carolina aside. "Please be careful," he told her; then he kissed her goodbye.

With the blood of gypsies that had been passed down from generations before her flowing in her veins, and because she was the daughter of the *Kaulo Camio choovihni*, Carolina now knew that the journey she and the FIGs were embarking on was no longer just a search for Dara's mother; it was a matter of life and death, good and evil. She knew it just as sure as she knew Larry was terrified for them. And because they were the Females of Intellectual Genius, Dara, Mackenzie and Jennifer knew it, too.

Embracing him one last time, Carolina walked through the boarding gate to join her three young charges.

CHAPTER NINE

The noise and confusion inside the terminal at LaGuardia on their arrival was almost unbearable. Mackenzie, being the problem-solver, was the first to come up with a plan—such as it was. "We need to find our luggage, then we will figure out what to do after that." Carolina and the other two young women agreed. Between the four of them, and by asking a lot of questions each time they saw an airport employee, they managed to find their way to the luggage carousel. There, they huddled together so as not to get separated as they watched each piece of luggage pass by on the conveyer belt. Jennifer's suitcase was the first to come into view, followed by Dara's. Finally Mackenzie's and Carolina's suitcases arrived. Everything seemed to be going according to plan until they realized they didn't know how to find Mr. Grai. However, that problem also was soon solved when a large sign with the letters F I G S printed boldly on it in black poked up above the mêlée and moved toward them. Mr. Grai, it seemed, had found them. Along with the sign he was dragging a luggage cart. Tall and thin, with dark curly hair, he could have passed for Larry's brother. As soon as he saw Carolina and her girls, he smiled broadly.

"Mr. Grai," said Carolina extending her hand, thrilled beyond words that things were working out as they should. She had been reprimanding herself only moments earlier for being so unprepared and ill equipped. But, as usual, Larry had thought of everything including giving Mr. Grai their flight information.

"Just Grai," he answered, "and you must be Carolina. Then looking at the three young women nearby, "and you are the FIGs. Welcome to New York." In all of the commotion of passengers gathering luggage, announcements blasting over loudspeakers, crying children, various cell phone ring tones assaulting them from every direction, and everyone rushing about, his smile and presence was calming and reassuring. The four young women felt safe and protected. This man with only one name would take care of them.

After loading their assortment of bags onto the cart, they pushed their way as a single unit through the crowd until they reached an exit. Once outside, Grai expertly loaded them and their luggage into his cab, which was convenient and considerably larger than Larry's car. Carolina hadn't realized until then that the "guy" Larry knew was a cab driver. Within minutes, they had left the airport behind and were traveling at a rapid speed toward the city. "You are going to really like staying with Mrs. Killebrew," he said. "She has been operating her boarding house for going on thirty years now. Her husband passed on about five years ago, but she decided she wanted to keep doing what she loved. Of course, she had to hire a couple of people to help her, but she still does all of the cooking." He glanced at Carolina sitting next to him, and then into the rearview mirror at the FIGs. "Let's see, this is Friday, so she will be fixing meatloaf. Believe me, it is the best you have ever tasted." This man with the friendly demeanor and a relaxed gift of gab smiled now, and once again glanced into the rearview mirror, this time looking directly at Dara.

Mackenzie noticed and giggled. Dara also caught his look. "Grai is the Romani word meaning horse," she said. When Carolina had first told the FIGs about him, she had pronounced his name as "Gray." Now seeing it written on the permit along with his photo on the dashboard of the cab, she realized it was spelled "Grai."

His eyebrows shot up and his smile widened. "That's right." But he didn't offer any other explanation, instead turning his attention to the increase in city traffic.

As a young child traveling with her parents, Jennifer had been to New York City many times. She was familiar with the sights, sounds, and smells of the Big Apple, but for Mackenzie, Dara, and Carolina, it was overwhelming. More than once Carolina stifled a scream, clenched her fists and ducked her head, thinking they were headed for a multi-car collision and certain death. Mackenzie didn't dare say anything, knowing if she did, no one would be able to understand her anyway because of her lisp. Dara just seemed lost in her cwn world. Feet planted firmly in front of her and knees together, she looked out the window at the disappearing scenery and people as the cab sped along.

Somewhere the Grand Central Expressway they were on merged into the Whitestone Expressway taking them across the Whitestone Bridge. "We are almost there," Grai offered, as he turned onto I-678 and then I-95. Finally they reached the Bronx and within minutes were parked in front of a well-kept brown-brick two-story house with a dark gray shingled roof, one of several on a narrow tree-lined street. Zinnias grew in abundance along the front of the house and flanked the wide stone steps leading up to the porch. A large wooden sign let them know that they had arrived at *Mrs. Killebrew's Boarding House.*

If it hadn't been for Grai helping her, Carolina would have fallen out of the cab into a heap. As it was, she managed, as did Dara, Mackenzie, and Jennifer. "Let's go in and let Mrs. Killebrew know you are here," Grai said. "She's looking forward to meeting you, and she won't like it if we are late. Then I'll see to your luggage." Again Carolina felt grateful that this man was there to help them. With everything happening so fast, she felt a little lost and a lot vulnerable, not to mention totally ill-equipped. The nail-biting, gut-wrenching drive from the airport hadn't helped. She hoped her girls weren't feeling the same way.

Carolina and the three Females of Intellectual Genius followed the tall, thin man with dark curly hair up the front porch steps and into a cool foyer decorated with late Victorian furniture, lace curtains, and an eclectic mix of antiques. It was the place they would call home for the next few weeks.

They barely got inside when a portly, white-haired woman wearing a pink print dress protected by an apron with the words "Hot Stuff" printed on the front bustled into the foyer where they were waiting. "There you are," she said putting her hands on her broad hips and glaring at Grai. Then, "Did he take good care of you?" she asked, looking at Carolina and the FIGs and obviously assessing them. The small wire-framed glasses she was wearing had slipped down on her nose. Carolina assured her that he had. Leading the new arrivals up some stairs located in a central hallway, she showed her guests where they would be staying.

The rooms were large and, like the foyer downstairs, beautifully decorated with Victorian furniture and antiques. They each had a room with a window covered in lace overlooking the back, away from the street and traffic noise, and the rooms all adjoined. They would share one large bathroom that had probably been modernized a few years back and was now complete with a clawed-foot tub, a walk-in shower, a commode, and a double sink.

"This is perfect, Mrs. Killebrew," Carolina told her hostess. "It is just beautiful."

"Well, you just make yourselves right at home." Just then Grai came in with several pieces of luggage, then left to go get the rest. As the girls started sorting and placing each bag according to its owner, Mrs. Killebrew planted herself in front of Carolina. "You girls need to know that we do have house rules here. No loud music after 10 at night. That is also when I lock up, so if you are planning to be out later than that, you will need to get a key ahead of time. Otherwise you will have to sleep on the porch. If you use the washer and dryer, clean the dryer filter after each use. Mrs. Rothstern comes in every Wednesday to clean and vacuum, so don't leave anything on the floor. We eat breakfast at 7, dinner at noon, and supper at 6—promptly," she continued. "Since we eat our main meal at noon, supper is just soup and sandwich or something light. And I do serve leftovers," she warned. "Do you have any questions?" she asked on her way back down the stairs. Even if they had, they wouldn't have dared to ask. "Dinner will be ready in half an hour. So you have time to get settled in and relax a bit. The dining room is downstairs off to the left of the hall where you came in. Just come on down when you are ready. If you are late, you don't get anything to eat!" This last warning was yelled from the bottom of the stairs.

Grai came in with the rest of their luggage. "She's harmless," he whispered, glancing toward the stairs to make sure he hadn't been overheard. Then he, too, disappeared back down the stairs.

Carolina, Dara, Mackenzie, and Jennifer stood looking at one another, not moving and wide-eyed, and then Mackenzie giggled. Jennifer flipped her ponytail and picked up her shoulder bag, checking it to make sure her portfolio of blank, eight-stave paper and sketch pad were still safe. Dara trolled around the rooms they would be staying in, touching an old framed photo of a short man and an even shorter woman who vaguely resembled Mrs. Killebrew —maybe Mr. and Mrs. Killebrew when they were young, admiring the colorful zinnias that had been placed in each of the rooms—taken from those she had noticed growing in the yard most likely, examining a doily on the back of a blue velvet, over-stuffed chair—probably handmade, making herself familiar with her surroundings.

"I must say, I think I know how Dorothy felt when she and Toto got picked up and blown away by that tornado. We are definitely not in Kansas anymore," said Carolina watching Dara.

"Which room do you want, Dara?" asked Mackenzie, surprised that her friend hadn't already picked it out. But Dara didn't answer. She was looking again at the photo of the young man and woman, lost in her own world, her own thoughts.

"I'll take this room, and Dara can have the one right next to it," Carolina said noticing the concern on Mackenzie's face. "Come on, Dara," said Carolina picking up her suitcase, "let's get settled in so we can go have some of that terrific meatloaf."

For the next half hour, they unpacked, washed up, and explored. The house was much larger than it appeared from the front, and there were several other bedrooms on the second floor, all empty, and located across from their rooms on the other side of a long hall. Carolina made a quick call to Larry and left a message letting him know they had arrived, they were safely installed in Mrs. Killebrew's boarding house, and that she would call him later that evening.

By the time they found the dining room, they really were famished since they had left Wood Rose that morning before breakfast and hadn't eaten anything on the flight. Apparently they were the only ones staying with Mrs. Killebrew; at least no one else joined them for dinner, other than Grai. By the end of the meal, they had decided that Mrs. Killebrew's meatloaf was the most delicious meatloaf they had ever eaten. Dara seemed to be feeling better, and when Grai offered to take them on a "quick tour" around the Big Apple that afternoon, it was she who decided that might be best. They would start the search for her mother the next day.

As Carolina and the FIGs rode through the streets of the city, craning their necks to see the Empire State Building, Central Park, the Metropolitan Museum, and then later the Statue of Liberty—"just a few of the highlights for you to explore later when you have time," Grai told them, hidden deep within the dark bowels of the earth, below the rumble and screeching of trains and the crush of humanity, away from all that gives hope to life, in a secret, silent shadow world, a single red light blinked impatiently on the muted telephone, immediately stopping when the receiver was lifted. "She is here." Quietly, the receiver was replaced.

CHAPTER TEN

*T*he *Kaulo Camioes* were well on their way when the first rays of sunlight filtered through the dense trees spreading shadows across the road on which they travelled. They would travel until the heat of late day became too intense on the younger children. Then they would stop for the night.

Lyuba rode alone in her wagon, slightly separated from the others. She preferred it that way. There was much to think about, and the constant, frivolous chatter of the other women only served as an annoyance and distraction. More often than not they were getting turned away by the settled population. There were fewer places for them to stop overnight, much less stay for any period of time. Estrangement was causing distrust, and distrust fear of the travelers. "They are from the lost continent of Atlantis," some of the settlers said. "They are the last of the priestly caste of the old Egyptian religion, forced out by the New Order," said others. There had even been an archaeological study done linking the DNA between present-day European gypsies to the ancient tribes from India. The settled people didn't understand what the gypsies knew: That there have always been the travelers since the beginning of time, and there would be travelers until the end of time, no matter what the *gorgia* believed.

In a few days they would arrive in Frascati. Less than 10 kilometers south of Rome, it was the nearest of the Castelli towns. As in times past, the gypsies would camp on a hill nearby, once called Tusculum by the ancients, in the shadows of the Villa Mondragone, so named because of the many dragons carved in its brown stone edifice. The gypsies simply called it the Old Villa. Originally built on Roman ruins in the sixteenth century, it had survived through the centuries as home to various Catholic cardinals and periods of abandonment until most recently when it had been sold by the college of the Jesuits to the Second University of Rome. From their camp, it was an easy walk into Frascati, a rural village not yet marred by tourism. The villagers still held on to some of the old beliefs, making it easier for the gypsies to sell their wares. But even in Frascati, there was the foul scent of change. Lyuba had noticed it when they were last there; the others who had been there before did as well. Soon it would become a destination for tourists, with its fancy wine and its historical villa. It was inevitable.

The contentment Lyuba had been feeling in recent days had diminished somewhat since seeing the single magpie. Her reading of the Tarot the night before had not given her the answers she sought; only that she needed to be aware and that danger was near. The answers would eventually be revealed to her, but until then there was nothing she could do.

The heat from the late afternoon sun was getting strong. Soon they would have to stop. Thankfully, it had been a good day with no mishaps. She would give her blessing once they settled in for the night. Glancing up into sky, she noticed the thunderheads starting to gather in the north from where they had just traveled. They had not broken camp too soon.

CHAPTER ELEVEN

After eating a meatloaf sandwich and a bowl of homemade chicken noodle soup for supper later that evening—"so you keep your energy up and the germs away—we do not need diseases or shin splints," Mrs. Killebrew told them— the three FIGs gathered in Carolina's room to discuss strategy and how to go about their search for Dara's mother. Grai had told them that he was available to take them anytime and anywhere they needed to go. Now they just needed to decide how best to approach the five women on the list.

"I think we should just start with the first name on the list and then work down," said Dara. Mackenzie and Jennifer were glad she spoke up first and seemed to be more herself. They were more comfortable with her taking the lead.

"I agree," said Jennifer, flipping her ponytail and looking at Mackenzie who nodded.

"That's what we'll do then," said Carolina. "I'll tell Grai that we will be ready to go right after breakfast." They had learned over soup and sandwiches that evening that Grai also lived at the boarding house, and that he was one of the "couple of people" Mrs. Killebrew had hired to help out after her husband died. The other person was the woman Mrs. Killebrew had already mentioned—Mrs. Rothstern, a strong, middle-aged woman who came in on Wednesdays and did all of the cleaning. "I just can't climb all of those stairs like I once could," Mrs. Killebrew told them.

One by one Carolina and the FIGs got ready for bed. Thinking ahead, Carolina knew that the next several days, maybe weeks, were going to be rough. As strong as Dara was, even she had a breaking point. Dara was good at keeping her defenses up and her insecurities and fears hidden, but Carolina recognized the signs.

She had already glimpsed a little bit of it earlier that day in the young woman who normally presented herself so aggressively. Dara would reach that point when everything would seem so overwhelming and unreal that she would feel totally helpless—unable to think or to act, and wanting only to disappear. Carolina had reached her breaking point two days after she found out she had been adopted. Not the day she learned about it, but two days later. She didn't want to see anyone, talk to anyone, or be around anyone. She was convinced she was a failure. It was as though her entire life had been made up of deceit and lies. She'd never been completely comfortable around the people she had been living with anyway, and when she found out she was adopted, she felt like she didn't even know herself. She didn't trust herself to be able to make decisions or know the difference between what was real and what was not. It was the small wooden box—her special treasure—that gave her the most comfort during that time, and gradually she pulled herself out of the darkness.

Dara's situation was different, though. She remembered her mother and she knew the circumstances that led to her going to live in an orphanage; that her mother had abandoned her when she was only seven years old. That must have been terribly difficult to deal with early on. How could a little girl possibly understand and live with that kind of pain? That same knowledge, however, was what made Dara the strong young woman she was today. But Carolina was worried about her. And no matter what, she would be there to help her get through it, just as she knew Mackenzie and Jennifer would be. Just as they had been for her.

***

At first Dara didn't turn out her light, preferring instead to study the wallpaper in the room where she was sleeping, between Carolina's room and Mackenzie's room. Just like the flowers in the vase next to her bed, flowers in colors of deep burgundy, yellow, and blue—jewel tones—floating on a background of ecru were displayed in large beautiful bouquets tied with lavender silk ribbons. She was reminded of the room she and the FIGs had shared when they stayed with Mother and Papa Granchelli. The wallpaper in that room had flowers, too— large, yellow cabbage-patch roses; and also, just like that room that had been chosen especially for them, the rooms they were staying in now had been chosen especially for them.

Her eyes drifted to the small table next to her bed and the things on it: the vase of flowers, a lamp that had two amber glass globes, a pretty ceramic dish, a small book of verse written by various women poets. She picked up the book and glanced at the names listed alphabetically: Bella Akhmadulina, Anna Bunina, Willa Cather, Emily Dickinson. Then, because it was what she did whenever she faced an especially challenging situation, she focused on words, or in this case, the family surnames of women poets, first establishing the root of each main word, or symbol in some instances, and assigning it a certain "weight" or number to determine its origin.

She was tired, having not slept in several nights. As she looked at the names in the small leather-bound book, placing the female poets' origins in countries such as France, Russia, and China, she realized that the reason she hadn't slept was because of something she had never been able to admit to anyone, not even to Mackenzie and Jennifer. Not even Carolina. Something she hadn't even been able to admit to herself because of the overwhelming guilt associated with it. But there in the beautiful room that had been picked out just for her, with the wallpaper covered in bouquets of flowers tied with silk ribbons, and at just that moment, she was somehow able to confront it at least in her thoughts.

She hated her mother.

For leaving her that day in the candy shop and not coming back. For not loving her daughter enough to keep her. Even though they didn't have much, it had been enough for Dara. Apparently it wasn't enough for her mother, though.

Dara had overcome so much: feelings of inadequacy, of failure, afraid of never being able to amount to anything. Of never being wanted by anyone. It was her genius with foreign and obscure languages that had sustained her through the years. It was also her genius that gave her permission to bury the feelings of hate for her mother so deep that they could never surface. But now, after all this time, facing the prospect of seeing the woman she had loved and called mama, that hatred had risen from the depths of her soul and resurfaced.

And she felt guilty.

***

Once the house got quiet and she thought everyone was asleep, Mackenzie sat up, fluffed her pillow behind her back, and pulled the little gold chain that turned on the white, hobnail glass lamp next to her bed. Then she reached for the small computer that was never far away, which applied logarithms and other difficult mathematical calculations and stored information, and began methodically punching in figures. Even as unrelated and disconnected everything seemed to be, there was a certain mathematical logic to it. There always was, for numbers never lied.

Five different addresses from five different areas of the city; yet they were an equal distance from the center—the center being Grand Central Terminal. It was more than just a strange coincidence, as Larry had said. More than likely he just didn't want them to worry. There had to be a logical reason for it. And what did the number "61" have to do with everything?

Mackenzie pulled up another app she had installed on her computer before leaving Wood Rose that gave a lot of the history of Grand Central Terminal and the area that surrounded it. She also wanted to research the five addresses as well and had downloaded documents she had found in public records. The first address they were going to the next morning was in an older part of the city, she quickly discovered, but the apartment building itself was fairly new. The original building had been destroyed by fire several years back. She tried to pull up a tenant list to see if she could get any background information on who lived there, now as well as before the building burned, but hit a dead end.

The excitement of the past twenty-four hours and her concern for Dara suddenly left her feeling exhausted. She once again pulled the little gold chain; and tiptoeing into Dara's room, quietly slipped into her friend's bed and immediately fell asleep. From the screen of the small computer left behind, next to the white, hobnail glass lamp, a faint light illuminated the number "61."

***

As soon as Jennifer went to her room, she pulled out her portfolio of blank, eight-stave paper and artist pad and climbed into bed. The black and white image had returned during supper, this time with some color—a broad horizontal streak of brilliant red. A splash of bright yellow. And along with the red and yellow was a beat—insistent, demanding. Pulling out a sheet of her drawing paper, Jennifer quickly started sketching the image: swirls of fog and smoke, the brilliant streak of red. When she did, the notes started to reveal themselves—tentatively, *pianissimo,* and without expression. Grabbing a sheet of her eight-stave paper, she rapidly began writing down the notes until there were no more.

The stone in her chest had gotten large again. She folded her arms tight against her, trying to ease the pain. When that didn't work, she threw back the covers and went to Dara's room where she knew she would find her two best friends. Crawling into bed with them, she turned on her side, her foot touching another, reaching for a hand. Lying down next to Dara and Mackenzie helped to ease the pain—a little; the stone was getting smaller again.

Soon the pain would disappear, and when it did, Jennifer would sleep.

***

The storm was moving south much quicker than had been originally forecasted. And it was gaining in strength. Reports of potential flooding reached the tribe. The Bandoleer decided that the *Kaulo Camioes* would take fewer breaks during the day and travel late into the evening, thus staying ahead of the worsening weather system. It would be difficult on the younger children, but that was better than getting caught in a severe storm with no shelter. With only the light from lanterns lit with kerosene hanging from each wagon to guide them, the travelers carefully made their way over the rough roads through the darkness of night.

Lyuba had been visited by the magpie again that morning. Once they stopped for the night, she would study the Tarot to see if more revelations would appear to her. She had made a small offering—a hair pin—in the nearby stream where they had stopped the night before asking for the blessing of safe travel. She would do the same on this night.

CHAPTER TWELVE

The next morning Carolina was happy to see the FIGs looking so rested. And after eating the wonderful breakfast Mrs. Killebrew had prepared for them, they seemed ready to take on whatever was presented to them—good or bad. By the time Grai made an appearance, the four young women were already waiting for him outside.

Carolina had written out the address for Grai, and before going down for breakfast Mackenzie had pulled it up on a map displayed on her small computer giving directions as well—just in case.

"Well, that's interesting," Grai said when he saw the address.

"What is interesting?" asked Carolina. The three FIGs sat forward in the backseat.

"If that is the area I think it is, all of those apartment buildings were torn down a couple of years ago to make way for a new land development project. I think it is under construction now, so we probably can't even get in there."

That didn't quite fit in with what Mackenzie had read about it. Rather than say anything, she removed her small computer from her waistband and placed it on her lap where she could keep an eye on where Grai was taking them. Jennifer and Dara noticed, and because they were Females of Intellectual Genius, they knew not to say anything either. "Let's try anyway," Dara said. She knew that Mackenzie had already researched the area where they were going. In fact, Mackenzie had told them that morning when they were dressing about the apartment building that had burned down, but a new one had been built. Grai might be a cab driver and know the city, but he could be mistaken. On the other hand, Mackenzie, Dara knew, wasn't mistaken because she was the problem-solver and a genius with calculus, algebra,

79

algorithms, geometry, and numerical codes. She wondered what Larry had told Grai about their visit. She was positive Carolina hadn't told him anything other than they would need for him to take them to several locations. And Jennifer and Mackenzie certainly hadn't said anything. Dara glanced up at the rearview mirror. Grai was watching her.

Between the up-town, mid-town, cross-town, and down-town traffic, it took them three hours to get to the address they were searching for. When Carolina realized they weren't going to get back to the boarding house in time for dinner, she timidly called Mrs. Killebrew to let her know. There were five apartment buildings, each eight stories high, built side by side. Four of them looked as though they had been around a long time. The one on the end, however, had been built more recently. "Let's stop there," said Dara pointing to the last building.

"Would you like for me to go with you?" Grai asked as he parked the cab and glanced around. The area didn't look that unsafe, but it wasn't the greatest either, and you just couldn't be too careful.

"No, but thank you," Carolina said, hoping she didn't sound too curt. After all, he was only trying to be helpful.

Grai nodded and waited as the four young women went to the main entrance. The front door was locked, but there was a bank of call buttons with the names of the residents on a panel next to the front door. Pearlee Devoraux Roux lived on the fourth floor in apartment 3. Since only Jennifer had visited New York previously, the others turned to her to negotiate the button call system. She pushed the button for Pearlee Devoraux Roux and, amazingly, they heard the front door lock disengage. Flipping her ponytail back and forth, something she usually did whenever she felt a keen sense of accomplishment, she opened the door wide for Carolina and the other FIGs to enter.

Once inside they found themselves in a lobby of sorts with beige walls and no furniture or decorations of any kind. There was also no elevator, at least none that they could find. So the four of them climbed the four flights of stairs, pausing on each landing to look out the window and catch their breath. Apartment 3 was easy enough to find, and Dara, because she always went first, walked up to the door and knocked.

From inside came the cries of a baby, soothing words spoken in French, and then the sound of several locks being turned and bolts being slid aside in order to open the door. By the time the door opened, Carolina and the FIGs were standing so close to one another, they almost appeared as one person. Carolina put her arm around Dara's shoulders.

"We are looking for Pearlee Devoraux Roux," Dara said to the young white woman holding a baby.

"Oui," the young woman answered.

Dara immediately began speaking to her in French. Was there someone else there named Pearlee Devoraux Roux—perhaps a little older? There was not. Did she know of anyone else named Pearlee Devoraux Roux who was African American—perhaps living in one of the other apartment buildings? She did not.

Dara thanked the woman and the four of them, Carolina and the FIGs, walked back down the four flights of stairs and out the door to the waiting cab. By then it was already getting late and they would need to start back if they were going to make it back to Mrs. Killebrew's in time for supper. Strangely enough, it didn't take nearly as long to return to the boarding house as it had finding the apartment. The other strange thing was that it appeared that Grai had gone out of the way numerous times that morning in search of the apartment, when the map Mackenzie had pulled up on her small, hand-held computer showed it being pretty much a direct shot across town.

These were things Mackenzie would discuss with Carolina and the FIGs later in the privacy of their rooms. For now, Mrs. Killebrew had prepared the noon meal for supper since the young women hadn't been there to enjoy it at mid-day. It was her Saturday special of beef tips over rice. She had also baked a chocolate cake for dessert. "Just don't think I am going to do this again," snapped Mrs. Killebrew. "The noon meal is supposed to be eaten at noon!" Grateful for her kind consideration, Carolina and the FIGs, and Grai, ate their meal in the dining room furnished in late Victorian, an assortment of eclectic antiques, and large windows adorned with lace while listening to Mrs. Killebrew discuss the virtues of punctuality.

***

Later that evening Carolina studied the map on Mackenzie's small computer. The three of them—Dara, Mackenzie, and Jennifer—were piled on Carolina's bed with her in the middle. "So you see, Carolina, he could just as easily taken this road here"—she pointed—"and gotten to the apartment buildings in about thirty minutes—not three hours." She glanced at Carolina. "It was like he didn't want us to go there, especially after that story he told about the apartment buildings being torn down."

"He might have just gotten the address confused with some other apartment buildings," reasoned Carolina.

"Not only that," Jennifer flipped her ponytail, "when we were climbing those stairs I noticed out the window that he was talking on the phone."

"There's nothing wrong with that, Jennifer. Everyone talks on their phone, especially if they are just waiting around."

"Except he wasn't just talking," explained Jennifer. "He had gotten out of the cab and was pacing back and forth, yelling and thrashing his arms around."

"Oh." Carolina looked at the other two FIGs, a frown suddenly appearing on her face. "Probably just a quarrel with his girlfriend."

"And he is always staring at me," added Dara.

Carolina had noticed that, too, to the point that it had started to concern her. She wondered where his room was. He had told her that when Mrs. Killebrew hired him to do repairs and maintenance at the boarding house, she had offered him free room and board. But she and the FIGs had explored the entire second floor where their rooms were located, and the other rooms on that floor were unoccupied. Since it was a two-story house, that meant he might have a room downstairs where Mrs. Killebrew's bedroom was located, or he had a room up in the attic. Not that it should even matter, except for some reason she felt at that particular moment that it was important to know.

"Look, he found us and took care of us when we first got here. Right? We would probably still be standing in front of the luggage carousel at LaGuardia if it hadn't been for him." Carolina was trying to ease their concerns. "And, Larry is the one who got in touch with him, so he must be a friend or someone he trusts." The girls nodded. "That doesn't mean we can't keep vigilant, though," she quickly added, "as we always should."

The conversation turned then to the next address on the list. This one, according to the map Mackenzie produced on her small computer, was in a completely opposite direction from the apartment they had visited that day. Looking at the grid where Mackenzie had pinpointed each address, the first address had been on the top left corner of the square. This second address was located at a diagonal on the lower right corner of the square. Also according to Mackenzie's calculations, it shouldn't take them more than an hour to get there and find the place. It appeared to be an individual home in the middle of several others from what she could tell when she looked it up on Google.

Because this second address didn't seem to be that far from the boarding house, the four young women decided they should also go ahead and look for the third address as well; that is, if Dara's mother wasn't at the second address. The third address was the top right corner of the square on Mackenzie's grid. If neither of the two addresses worked out, that would leave the one on the bottom left corner of the square of Mackenzie's grid, and then the one in the very center.

Late into the night Carolina went into each of the other three bedrooms checking on her girls. Satisfied that they were asleep, she went back to her own room to call Larry. She wanted to find out more about this friendly, easy-going cab driver who had only one name. Before she could dial, though, her phone played the ring tone that was hers and Larry's favorite song. "I was just getting ready to call you," she told him when she answered.

CHAPTER THIRTEEN

$\mathcal{T}$he travelers were making excellent time, staying well ahead of the dangerous storm system that had ballooned in size to the extent that it now threatened all of northern Italy. With another weaker system blocking it temporarily, the storm was stationary for now, feeding off a smaller, colder system moving in from the Atlantic. It would soon start moving south again, however, bigger and stronger, and would cause much flooding. The International Weather Bureau had already started issuing alerts. By pushing on late into the night, the travelers would be able to reach Frascati in a day and a half—perhaps less if there were no mishaps.

The place where they finally stopped for the night was in a grove of trees, off the road, and partially protected by a grassy mound. The men cared for the animals while the women tended to the children and prepared food to eat. Just as she had done on the previous nights, Lyuba made her offering—this time two perfect leaves from a maple tree, with their identifiable five points, buried in the dark soil. Again she asked for the blessing of safe travel. She would do the same the next night, and the next—until they reached their destination.

Later, once again Lyuba studied the Tarot, presenting questions, seeking answers. She placed the cards one by one onto the black silk. Much to her surprise, they felt warm. The card showing strength appeared first; the High Priestess, indicating secrets not ready to be revealed; the Wheel of Fortune, indicating change; and then the card of Death, only in this case signifying the end of something in order to make room for something new. Then she placed down three more cards: the Tower meaning an unexpected blow; the Star of luck and hope for future happiness; and the last card, Temperance. She would need to be watchful and take special care. Relying on her instinctive psychic powers, she selected one final card from those which had not yet been chosen. It was the Seven of Wands. There were difficulties ahead requiring all of her endurance and strength to overcome.

Later, when she had finished her reading, she carefully returned the Tarot cards to the protective box where she kept them, wrapped in the black silk scarf. Only this time, unlike the previous nights, she now knew the meaning of the magpie's warning.

Early the next morning before daybreak, the travelers, each following the other, one by one left the grove protected by the grassy mound and continued on their way, determined to reach Frascati by nightfall. In the darkness of this morning, however, they were now one less; for Lyuba had left in the middle of the night.

***

All four young women were up early the next morning. Since Mrs. Killebrew didn't have breakfast quite ready, they went outside to sit in the comfortable worn-wooden rockers that had been placed on the wide spacious porch with hanging ferns and two concrete cherubs leaning against the newels of the front steps. The sun was creeping out from behind some dark clouds, promising to make it a blistering day.

"Larry says they were in school together," Carolina said, continuing the conversation they had started earlier when they were getting dressed.

"Yeah, but what school?" asked Mackenzie.

"Well, I assume he meant the University of North Carolina since that is where Larry got his undergraduate and graduate degrees." Then pausing, "But now that you mention it, I don't know if that is what he meant at all. I met Larry at the university when we were both in undergraduate school, and I don't ever remember even seeing Grai much less meeting him." Thinking back to their conversation the night before, she wished she had pushed for more answers, but Larry had started talking about the classes he was teaching and they didn't return to the subject of Grai.

Dara, feet firmly planted, knees together, started rocking the wooden ladder-back chair back and forth.

Jennifer flipped her ponytail. "It would be interesting to know what he majored in and how he wound up as a cab driver in New York City." She began rocking her chair in unison with Dara's. Soon all four rockers moved as one, each brilliant mind filled with anxious anticipation, thinking about what the day would bring.

Unlike the day before when it seemed that Grai had deliberately gone out of his way to not find the address they were looking for, on this morning he said he knew the location. He also knew a shortcut. Again Mackenzie placed her small computer in her lap displaying the map and directions. In less than thirty minutes Grai pulled up in front of a brownstone located in Manhattan. The address they were searching for was prominently displayed next to the front door along with a mezuzah.

"If you need me, I'll be right here," said Grai, this time not offering to go with them.

Carolina smiled and climbed out of the cab, along with the FIGs. As she had done the day before, Dara led the all-female consortium up the brown brick steps and knocked. In a few minutes a man with a high-pitched voice spoke from behind the closed door. "Who is it?"

Mackenzie's hazel eyes grew large, and Jennifer flipped her ponytail. Once again Carolina put her arm around Dara.

"Does Pearlee Devoraux Roux live here?" she asked.

There was a pause, then the door partially opened. Dara found herself towering over a small man wearing a maroon morning breakfast jacket with a gold paisley ascot and green silk pajama bottoms. He took a moment for his eyes to adjust to the brightness of the early morning light, then looked at each of the young women standing at his front door. Deciding they weren't muggers and he was safe from any serious bodily harm, he opened the door wider exposing the cool, rich interior. "She was the previous owner," he said. "She died a couple of years ago. That's when I bought this place."

Dara felt her knees weaken and her heart drop. Carolina squeezed her arm tightly around her as her own heart pounded.

"Do you know if she was African American?" asked Mackenzie. After all, if she wasn't African American, then she couldn't be Dara's mother.

"She was Chinese," the little man answered. "Her husband was from Argentina. They had a leather goods shop around the corner." Then looking at Dara, "Are you a relative?"

But Dara knew she wasn't. "No. Sorry to bother you."

"Okay," said Jennifer as they walked back to the cab. "Two down and three more possibilities to go." She glanced at Dara to make sure she was all right. She was glad that Carolina still had her arm around her.

"That was the first time I have ever seen someone in real life wearing an ascot," said Mackenzie giggling.

"I really liked those green silk pajama bottoms," said Dara, smiling for the first time since arriving in New York City. The woman who had lived at the brownstone and had died wasn't her mother. She hadn't found her yet, but that didn't mean she wouldn't.

Because of Grai's shortcut in finding the brownstone, they still had plenty of time to go to the third location and still get back to the boarding house in time for lunch—or dinner as Mrs. Killebrew called it. Mrs. Killebrew had told them over breakfast that she was fixing beef pot roast and all the fixins'.

The next address, the top right corner of the square on Mackenzie's grid, proved to be even more difficult to locate than the apartment the day before. Even though Mackenzie could locate the address on her map, there didn't seem to be any way to get to it. "We've got it surrounded," Grai said several times, obviously irritated, but each street he took would either be a dead end, or it would simply circle around until they were back to where they started. With the approach of noon, and still no success in finding the address, they decided to go back to the boarding house so as not in inconvenience Mrs. Killebrew or her pot roast. They would set out again after dinner.

Late that afternoon, they eventually parked in front of a large, modernist, tower-in-the-park style apartment complex, "probably built in the 1930s," Grai told them. "The New York City Housing Authority built several of these developments, and they are spread out across the city. Most of them have 1000 apartment units or more. Others have been abandoned or torn down."

Unsure they should get out of the cab, Carolina and the FIGs just stared at what looked like an ancient crumbling city within a city. Finally, because she always took the lead, Dara opened the door and got out. The other FIGs followed, as did Carolina. Together they approached the derelict building and walked toward a ripped screen door that was hanging by one hinge. They didn't make it to the front stoop, however, because a tall black man came outside before they could get there. "What do you want?" he barked.

Unwilling to be intimidated, Dara squared back her shoulders. "We are looking for Pearlee Devoraux Roux."

"She ain't here." The man turned to go back into the apartment.

"Does she live here?" Dara asked quickly.

"Ain't never heard of her," came the answer, and the man disappeared into the darkness behind the ripped screen door hanging by one hinge.

Still… Dara wanted to be sure. She hadn't come all this way to be turned away from the truth now. She marched up to the stoop and tapped on what was left of the dilapidated door. Startling her, the man's face appeared from the darkness within the apartment just inches from hers. "I told you, she ain't here."

"Was she ever here?" Dara asked, noticing his deep Southern accent. "I bet you come from Alabama, don't you? Somewhere along the Gulf?" she asked, trying to draw this man out. Her heart, mind, and soul begging.

He glared at her, distrustful. "Maybe. Who wants to know?"

Dara recognized what was driving this man. After all, she had been exposed to that same attitude when living with her mother in the back-bay area in Virginia. The less people had, the more distrustful they were. Protective of what little they did have, they were distrustful of the government and authority and driven by anger and the feeling of failure. She had been too young at the time to put it into words, but she intuitively understood nonetheless.

She decided to be completely honest. "Look, my mother left when I was seven years old. I am looking for her, and I was told she might be living at this address."

Carolina and the FIGs moved near Dara, as though by combining the strength of each one of them, it would give Dara the strength she needed; hoping the man would understand and perhaps be able to give her the information she so much wanted.

He hesitated, sizing up the situation, trying to decide if he could trust this young black woman. Then... "She don't live here no more. She moved out. Said she had a job somewhere in the city working for the government. That's all I know."

Dara almost wept. At least this was something. "Thank you," she said, her body trembling.

"How long ago did she move?" Mackenzie asked.

The man shook his head. "Two, maybe three weeks."

As the four young women turned to walk back to the cab, the man said to Dara, "You look just like her, you know."

Mackenzie gasped, and Jennifer flipped her ponytail. Dara just kept walking. She knew her mother was alive now. And she would find her no matter what it took.

CHAPTER FOURTEEN

S he had her favorite place where she searched for special herbs, the place where the energies were strongest. Surprisingly, it was the old church graveyard built on a slight mound just outside of the rural Italian village. A river ran nearby, and a tall, unkempt yew tree grew near the entrance to the graveyard, poisonous, but giving off positive energies. It was a place she knew well, having discovered it from a previous time many years ago. And even though it was still dark, this is where Lyuba went now, even before she set up her hut or unpacked her belongings. Before she rested. She knew there was no time to waste.

Lyuba walked determinedly on the dirt path bordered by overgrown weeds that were once part of a magnificent garden on the grounds of the Old Villa. She was looking for something special, and she knew where to find it.

As dawn gradually replaced the darkness, Lyuba knelt by the massive ancient live oak tree holding a single tiny blue flower. Because she was the *choovihni* for the *Kaulo Camio* gypsy tribe, her knowledge extended into the darkest reaches of time. She dug into the earth at the base of the tree until she uncovered the small stone—her good luck charm—still wrapped in the remaining fragments of white paper; an offering she had made to save her daughter from the terrible curse when the tribe had stayed near the Old Villa before. Now, she replaced the dirt-covered fragments of paper with a clean white piece and once again placed the stone in it. Only this time she included the little blue flower with the knowledge that it would only react to the bad, but provide strength to the good.

As she continued kneeling she scattered the bread she had brought with her and water from the nearby river. "Tree mother,

I feed you; feed me in return." She spoke the spell as it had been passed down to her from her mother, also a *choovihni* all those years ago, and her grandmother before that. "Tree mother, I quench your thirst; quench mine in return." She then returned the stone along with the tiny blue flower wrapped in clean white paper to the earth dug at the base of the tree, saying, finally, "Tree mother, I bring you a gift; bless me by protecting those I love in return." She put both hands on the tree. "Rain falls, wind blows, sun shines, grass grows." She repeated it three times and then walked away without looking back.

***

Even though Mrs. Killebrew made a valiant effort to engage Carolina and her girls in light-hearted conversation that consisted primarily of her asking them questions about where they went that day, there was little talk during super around the large dining table that evening. Although Grai certainly held up his end, describing in detail how he had repaired a stubborn leak under the kitchen sink a few days before the guests had arrived at the boarding house.

The roast beef sandwiches disappeared, and there was nothing left of the chocolate cake by the end of the meal, but Carolina and the three FIGs were deep in thought as to what to do next. The day had been momentous. With only two addresses left—the one located in the bottom left corner of the grid on Mackenzie's map, and the address in the very center of the square—there was now a very real possibility that Dara's mother would be living at one of them. That one of them was where she had moved to only recently.

Upstairs in their rooms, they quickly got ready for bed. Then, as on previous nights, they all gathered in Carolina's room, flopping on her bed to discuss their next move. Mackenzie had already researched the remaining address located in the bottom left corner of the square. It was another apartment, but it seemed to be located above a grocer at a busy intersection in Queens, one of the boroughs. And the other address—the fifth one in the center of the grid—she just couldn't figure out. Either it was incorrect, or Dara's mother was living at Grand Central Terminal.

"What do you think, Carolina?" asked Dara.

"Things will be revealed when and where they should," she answered, not having a clue where the words even came from because they certainly weren't what she had planned to say.

"Whoa, Carolina," said Jennifer. "That sounded like something Lyuba would say."

Carolina laughed. "It did, didn't it!" Still, the message had been loud and clear, and she had heard it. "I think we should continue with our original plan. Find the fourth address on Mackenzie's grid, and if Dara's mother isn't there, then we will have to figure out how to negotiate Grand Central Terminal."

"Sounds like a plan to me," said Mackenzie. Jennifer flipped her ponytail, and Dara stared at the "X" on Mackenzie's grid with the red dot in the middle.

***

Late into the night Jennifer continued writing down the notes of music she heard. She had already completed the sketch, in full color—the streak of red, some yellow, but mostly black and brown and gray. Angry, dangerous colors. And now, once again, the notes were revealing themselves in musical bars, phrases, and movements—like inflections in speech or paragraphs in a book. The dissonance was loud, strong and restless, with a dark shadowing of B flat minor. Soon it would be complete, and when it was, she would understand what it meant. For now, she would keep writing down the notes, as she heard them in her mind, on blank, eight-stave paper. Because that was what made her a genius.

***

Mackenzie punched in the numbers, this time using a completely different approach. She knew that Numerology was the belief in a divine, mystical or other special relationship existing between a number and some coinciding event. Using the words "Grand Central Terminal" as her base, she then applied Isopsephy, an ancient use of Numerology, by adding up the number values of the letters in a word to form a single number. The number that came up was "61."

Mackenzie put down her small calculator and stared at the beautiful walls covered in blue and yellow paisley, reminding her once again of Mother and Papa Granchelli, her second family. This was just too much of a coincidence. They would go to the apartment over the grocer in Queens the next morning after breakfast, but there was no doubt in Mackenzie's mind that Dara's mother was somewhere in the Grand Central Terminal. She didn't know why or how, but she was definitely there.

***

Dara lay on her back staring up at the ceiling. She wasn't sure she wanted tomorrow to come. It had been ten years. What if they found her mother? What would she say? *Hi, I'm the kid you left in the candy store ten years ago.* Or, because her memories were so few, she might ask, *Do you still burn that smelly kerosene in a big black pot to keep the snakes away?*

Would she even remember having a daughter named Dara, the little girl who played with strange words like they were her friends?

Would she still be pretty and paint her mouth red?

Would she think the daughter she left behind was pretty?

Dara closed her eyes, slowly drifting to sleep—*Or maybe they just want to leave the place where they are and the people they know and not ever be found again.* "You wait here, pretty girl…."

***

When Larry didn't answer after several tries, Carolina turned out the light, smoothed out her pillow, and pulled the sheet over her. It was late, so she didn't understand why he wasn't home. She played back the events of the day in her thoughts, pausing on the man who told them Pearlee Devoraux Roux had moved just recently. But it was what he said afterwards that was keeping Carolina awake. Dara looked just like her, he had said. It had to have been her mother, and they just missed her.

Her heart was breaking for Dara knowing how she must feel. But tomorrow they would keep searching, and they would find her either at the apartment over the grocer in Queens, or somewhere in Grand Central Terminal. Which made absolutely no sense at all—unless she was homeless. But the man had said she had a government job working in the city. *Things will be revealed when and where they should.*

Carolina sighed, then turning her thoughts to dinner that evening, hoped Mrs. Killebrew didn't think they were rude for being so quiet. At least she had been able to find out that Grai owned his cab and only drove it part-time—which might explain why he got so lost that first day, although it didn't explain his heated argument over the phone Jennifer had observed.

Carolina had also learned that he had a room in the back of the house on the first floor. "Grai is also my security guard in addition to being my handyman, so it makes sense for him to be on the first floor to keep an eye on things in case there is any trouble," Mrs. Killebrew told her. "You just can't be too careful these days. There is all kinds of meanness out there."

Knowing that Grai had his room downstairs made Carolina feel a little better. Maybe she was just being paranoid when it came to the FIGs. And, after all, he had been a school chum of Larry's—wherever that was.

She picked up the phone again and dialed. After the sixth ring and still no answer, she put away her phone.

***

Larry rushed into his apartment, slamming the door behind him, flipped on the lights and grabbed his phone off the sofa where he had left it. At the last minute, a colleague had gotten an extra ticket to the Carolina Mudcats' home game in Zebulon. In his haste, he had left his cell phone behind.

The log showed six missed calls, all from Carolina. He checked his watch—it was already past midnight. As luck would have it, the game had gone into extra innings. Rather than wake her, he decided to call her first thing in the morning, angry at himself for being so forgetful.

CHAPTER FIFTEEN

*L*yuba watered the big brown horse with the mark of the pentacle of Solomon on its forehead, then tethered it in the deep grass where he could feed near some shade as the first rays of sun spilled over the horizon. He had worked hard to get her to this place where she needed to be. If all went well, the *Kaulo Camioes* would arrive late that evening. She had already made her offering asking for their safe travel.

She would set up her hut in the shadows of the Old Villa later, at the same spot she had stayed on previous visits. Even though it was still early, she knew they would already be up. The farm animals required it. She would wash the dust of travel from her body and rest later as well. Now she must go to the Granchelli farm. The zee presented itself in many shapes and forms. Lyuba knew them all—the energy of both animate and inanimate life: when to feel sadness, when to feel happiness, and when to feel fear. What she felt now was overwhelming fear.

Lyuba tucked the *parik-til* she had prepared especially for Mrs. Granchelli into her pocket. She also took the other *parik-til* because she knew she would see the other woman—Lucia—as well. Looking up at a nearby tree, once again the magpie appeared—quiet, watching her, warning her. She must not delay any longer. Walking quickly, she made her way through the tall weeds toward the Granchelli farm.

***

The song that Carolina and Larry considered their own brought Carolina out of a deep sleep. It took her a moment to remember where she was and then she had to find her phone. By

97

the time she did, it had stopped ringing. It immediately started ringing again.

"Larry, where were you last night?" Carolina asked pushing herself up into a sitting position. "I was worried."

"I am so sorry," he said, then went on to explain about the baseball game and extra innings. "But, enough of that, how did yesterday go? Did you find out anything else about Dara's mother?"

Carolina told him about what they had learned, and that they planned to start looking for the last two addresses on the list as soon as they had breakfast. "The really odd thing, though, is that one address we told you about that seems to be the Grand Central Terminal. There isn't anything else around there but the Terminal itself."

Larry had no idea what that could mean. Only that they should be extremely careful. "We don't know what kind of woman Dara's mother is or what she has been doing these past ten years," he said, "assuming you are even able to find her. Just be careful," he repeated.

Before hanging up, Carolina remembered to ask him about where he and Grai had gone to school together, "just out of curiosity," she said, hoping she didn't sound suspicious.

Larry knew the question would eventually get asked. "We are from the same tribe of travelers and were taught by the same *choovihni*. Just as I did, Grai also decided at a young age to lead a life separate from the gypsy culture, and when he was old enough he moved to New York where he attended New York University. His undergraduate degree was in public service, and he later went to law school as well." Then, sensing that Carolina needed to be reassured, "He is a good, honest man, Carolina. He has the instincts of a gypsy, and I trust him."

That answered the question of where Larry and Grai went to school together, but it didn't answer the question of why Grai was a cab driver and handyman-security guard with an advanced degree in law. "So why does he..." Just then the FIGs tapped on her door and peeked in. "Are you awake?" Carolina smiled and motioned for them to come in. She would have to ask later. "Tell them I said 'hi,'" said Larry. "I'll talk to you later."

***

Being that it was Sunday morning, there wasn't the usual traffic to deal with, and Grai was able to drive to the address they had written down for him in less than an hour even though it was farther away from the boarding house than the other addresses had been. Also, because it was Sunday, the grocery store was closed. Carolina and the FIGs looked through the shop windows of Woo-sung's Grocery to see if perhaps anyone was inside working, but saw no one. Then they walked around the building looking for another entrance leading to the upstairs apartment.

The store was located on the corner of an intersecting east-west street and north-south avenue, and on the east side of the building they found a door. There was also a buzzer. Once again, as she had done at the large, eight-floor apartment building, Jennifer pressed the buzzer. Rather than the door unlocking, however, this time they heard a man's voice over a speaker. Carolina, Jennifer, and Mackenzie didn't understand what the man was saying, but Dara did, and she began talking to him in Korean.

"There is no one here by that name," she translated for the others. "This has been his place of business and home for the past twenty years."

"Ask him if he ever employed anyone by that name," suggested Mackenzie.

Dara again spoke in Korean. Then, shaking her head, "No... wait!" Again the man was speaking to her. Dara looked at the others. "He says there was a girl who helped out occasionally over the holidays. Just part time. He says her name was Pearl. But she quit so she could move to California to be closer to family."

Dara asked him more questions, but either he didn't want to give out any additional information or he just didn't know.

"Ask him how old she was," said Jennifer. At least that way they would know if they should try to locate her in California or eliminate her altogether.

"He says she was young—about sixteen or seventeen. She had run away from home, but then decided to go back to her family. I guess that explains why she used this address as her own. She probably didn't have any place else."

Dara thanked him and turned to the others. "Well, I guess that leaves the dot in the middle—Grand Central Terminal," referring to the grid Mackenzie had drawn. The four young women—Carolina and the FIGs—stood looking at one another, not saying anything and not moving, yet they all felt it. Because Dara, Mackenzie, and Jennifer were Females of Intellectual Genius, and because Carolina was the daughter of the *Kaulo Camio choovihni* and had the blood of gypsies that had been passed down from generations flowing in her veins, they knew that they were about to face something they didn't understand nor could they prepare for; something that if they survived it, it would change their lives forever. The words—*Things will be revealed when and where they should*—filled Carolina's thoughts, pushing away all others. And then she heard, *I am here with you, my precious daughter. Take care.*

Grai, concerned that the young women were taking so long, got out of his cab to go see if anything was wrong. He stopped when he saw them walking his way. Determined, with no thoughts of turning back, they silently got into the cab. They would go back to the boarding house in time to eat Mrs. Killebrew's Sunday dinner special—fried chicken and mashed potatoes with gravy, she had told them that morning. After that, they would get Grai to take them to Grand Central Terminal and face whatever they had to face.

CHAPTER SIXTEEN

With a sense of urgency and determination, Lyuba knocked on the beautiful door made of old oak and hand-rubbed with the oil of olives and scented with lemon to create a rich dark luster. She heard the heavy footsteps of Mrs. Granchelli, probably preparing breakfast in the kitchen. Mr. Granchelli would already be out in the barn feeding the chickens and milking the cows. The footsteps came closer and then the door opened.

It took Mrs. Granchelli a moment to recognize this woman, dressed in all black—but only a moment. "Lyuba, you have come back!" The large Italian woman reached for the tall, thin gypsy and hugged her, then leading her into her home, "Come in. I am just fixing breakfast. Papa has gone out to get some fresh eggs."

Just then Mr. Granchelli came in with a basket full of eggs. "The girls did well," he said, smiling and holding up the basket, but then he saw Lyuba. "Well, my goodness, look who's here." He also hugged the gypsy woman and pulled out a chair from the kitchen table for her to sit in. "Has your tribe come back to camp at the Old Villa?"

"Yes, they are on their way," Lyuba answered, "but I come to you on an urgent matter."

Fresh eggs and breakfast forgotten, Mother and Papa Granchelli sat across the table from Carolina's mother and listened with concern as she told them she needed their help. Lyuba's daughter and those beautiful young women who had stayed with them during the summer were in danger. Lyuba needed to try to call Carolina, to warn her, but she had no phone. In fact, she wouldn't have known how to use it even if she had.

Mother Granchelli took on the airs of a military general going into battle. After all, these four young women were like her

101

own children. "Papa, get my address book, quickly." Papa ran into another room and came back carrying a well-worn book brimming with loose pages. Mother Granchelli, adjusting her glasses, flipped through the pages until she found what she was looking for. The phone was hanging on the wall there in the kitchen, and she quickly dialed the number Carolina had left with her—the phone number that would reach her at her bungalow at Wood Rose Orphanage and Academy for Young Women. When there was no answer, she tried Carolina's cell phone but wasn't able to get through. Perhaps she had it turned off. That was when she called her good friend—a distant cousin actually—Signora Lucia De Rossa who was head of the Frascati Records Office and who had been involved with Carolina's adoption all those many years ago. It was Lucia who had helped Carolina find her birth mother. Maybe she would have a suggestion of how to reach Carolina.

In addition to the two numbers Mother Granchelli had already tried, Lucia had the telephone number of the administration offices at Wood Rose as well as the cell number for Carolina's young man, Larry Gitani. After giving Mother Granchelli both numbers, she told her assistant she had an emergency and quickly left her office. A short time later, she, too, was sitting at the large kitchen table with Mother and Papa Granchelli and Lyuba. Since she had a little bit better command of the English language than Mother and Papa Granchelli or Lyuba, "Perhaps I can help with the calls," she offered.

"Carolina's young man didn't answer when we called, but he might be teaching. So we called the orphanage—Wood Rose— and Lyuba spoke to a Mrs. Ball," Mother Granchelli told Lucia, "and she told Lyuba that Carolina and the FIGs are in New York. I wrote down where they are staying." She gave Lucia the piece of paper. "There is also a phone number," she said pointing.

Lyuba had gotten very quiet, and Mother Granchelli was concerned for this wise woman who possessed the knowledge of the ancient Romani. She had obviously been traveling all night, and she didn't look well. "Lucia, you call that number while I fix us something to eat." She poured a freshly-brewed cup of coffee for each of them, and set about cooking the eggs Papa had brought in earlier.

***

Mrs. Ball stood at the large window in the headmaster's office overlooking the *Photinia frasen* to see if he had left the cafeteria yet. Apparently there had been some sort of problem with the kitchen staff about an egg delivery, and he had gone over to get it sorted out. It had been such a strange phone call, the woman calling with an unusual accent and difficult to understand. And even though the caller hadn't said so, Mrs. Ball sensed it was urgent.

Normally she wouldn't give out information like that—ever! But there was something in the woman's voice that made her want to do all she could to help. She looked at her watch impatiently; he should have gotten everything squared away by now. After all, how much time could it take to settle an argument over the number of eggs ordered and the number that had gotten delivered?! If he didn't return soon, she would have to go find him. Just then she saw her boss, slightly stooped, with gray thinning hair, in his dark gray suit and conservative striped tie, striding down the walkway toward the administration building. She would tell him about the call and, hopefully, he would agree that she had done the right thing.

***

Larry had three student conferences scheduled between classes that afternoon, but he couldn't concentrate. Carolina had told him they were going to the last two addresses on the list that day. The one that concerned him was the fifth address that appeared to be Grand Central Terminal. Unless the woman was living there, which was impossible, it just didn't make sense. Yet he knew that Grai would never have included it on the list unless it was correct.

He glanced at his watch. The student was 10 minutes late. Just then his cell phone buzzed. He didn't recognize the number, but he did know the area code. It was a call from Italy.

"Larry Gitani," he answered.

A woman's voice spoke in broken English. "Larry, this is Lucia De Rossa." Then without waiting for his response, "It is urgent that Lyuba speak with you." She handed the phone to Lyuba, and for the next several minutes, the wise woman, with the knowledge of the ancient Romani passed down from her mother and her grandmother before that, spoke to the only son of the Gypsy King, the son who had left the gypsy culture, yet who had the instincts of his father, telling him of the warnings, revealing her fears, explaining what must be done. Her last words were, "There is no time left."

Larry rushed out of his office, nearly knocking down the student who was late for his appointment. "Reschedule," Larry yelled over his shoulder as he ran down the hall. He stopped by his apartment only long enough to pack a few things in a carry-on bag, then drove to the Raleigh-Durham International Airport. Within forty-five minutes of receiving the phone call, he was boarded on a flight heading for the LaGuardia Airport in New York. He had tried calling Carolina, but either she had her phone turned off, or she had left it somewhere. Or maybe she had simply forgotten to charge it, which she frequently did. He also tried calling Grai with no better result. He was able to talk to Mrs. Killebrew, but the only thing she knew was that Grai had taken the four young women out that afternoon as soon as they had finished dinner.

After two and a half hours, the plane landed. Again Larry tried calling Carolina, then Grai, with no success. Frustrated and trying desperately to control the panic he was feeling, he grabbed the first taxi he saw. "Grand Central Terminal," he told the driver.

CHAPTER SEVENTEEN

Before leaving, Lyuba gave Mother Granchelli and Lucia the special *parik-tils* she had prepared for each of them, made with gratitude and love and the wisdom of a *choovihni*. The *parik-tils* would protect them and give them good health. It was what Lyuba wished for them because these two settlers had given so much to her Carolina, and as a result, also to her. As different as their worlds were, they accepted her, and Lyuba would always hold them with love in her heart because of that.

Walking back to the Old Villa, Lyuba felt old and tired. She wasn't sure what she had done was enough to protect Carolina and her three young friends. Larry would be able to help, but would he get there in time? She watched for the magpie, but only heard its mournful cries off in the distance.

Back in the shadows of the Old Villa she set up her hut, positioning it beneath the trees so that it would receive an abundance of light, and arranged her herbs and bottles of oils where she knew they would receive the warmth of the early morning sun. Then she walked to the nearby river and washed the dust of travel from her skin. Later, she lay down on the many-colored quilt that had been sewn by her grandmother and softened by numerous washings and years of use. It would ease the worry in her soul, her spirit, and her mind and help her focus on what she must do next. A short while later, she got up and drank some hot tea she made from the root of the sassafras.

Lucia had said she would come to her if Larry were to get back in touch with them. Mother Granchelli has offered to let her stay with them until the others in her tribe arrived. But Lyuba could not. She needed to be in her own place and with her own things. She needed to prepare another offering, one that would ward off evil. Now that she was rested, she would return to the ancient live oak tree.

***

"You mean you gave her the phone number of where they are staying in New York?" The veins on Headmaster Harcourt's neck protruded and his eyes looked as though they might leave their sockets.

Mrs. Ball was mortified. In all of the years she had been employed at Wood Rose Orphanage and Academy for Young Women, not once had anything she had done ever been questioned. And she certainly had never been spoken to in such a disrespectful manner!

"You didn't even know who she was. Why on earth would you give out that kind of information about any of our students?"

"She said her name was Lyuba," Mrs. Ball replied somewhat forcefully. She had taken about all she was going to from this pompous, overweight know-it-all whom she had protected on numerous occasions because of his carelessness and outright stupidity. "And I felt that it was important—no, urgent! to give the information to her."

The headmaster knew he was approaching dangerous territory if he said anything else to Mrs. Ball in a critical way. And he really couldn't afford to have her upset with him. She knew way too much about him and about the things he had done on campus as headmaster. Nothing major, but numerous little things over the years that when added up would probably get him fired if the Board were to find out, or, at the very least, a real ass-chewing from Miss Alcott which would be even worse. "Here I thought we were going to have a nice, peaceful summer with the FIGs gone, but I should have known; nothing is ever peaceful where they are concerned. Is it?" He was trying to soften his tone and put himself back on her good side. Instead, she only sniffed and shuffled some papers before tossing them back on his desk without really straightening them. He made another attempt.

"Mrs. Ball, I am sure you felt you were doing the right thing by giving out that information to LouLou…"

"Lyuba," she interrupted, with a little more force and a hint of belligerence.

"Right. Lyuba." He sighed, feeling her glare rather than seeing it. Then, realizing it was going to take more, he buckled, "And I trust your judgment completely." He waited a moment to see if those words would have any positive affect. They did, for a very faint smile appeared on her lips. "After all, you were here to take the call, and I wasn't. I would never presume to question your judgment." The smile broadened just slightly. It wasn't exactly a smile, but at least the corners of her mouth were moving in an upward direction. Then, hoping that what he was now about to say wouldn't undo everything he had just said, "What would you think about calling that boarding house where they are staying and maybe just letting them know that Lou…"

"Lyuba!" Mrs. Ball practically yelled.

"Right, Lyuba was trying to get in touch with them and that you… we… gave her the phone number where they could be reached?"

"I already have. They weren't there, so I left a message," said Mrs. Ball walking out of the headmaster's office feeling completely venerated and totally justified.

Utterly exhausted to the point of being near a nervous breakdown, Headmaster Harcourt walked quickly to his large window to examine his prize *Photinia frasen,* as though somehow the strange phone call from a woman named LouLou, or whatever, had somehow caused it irreparable damage. Reassured that no harm had come to it, he collapsed onto the dark green sofa.

***

"I have already reserved a parking space near Grand Central Terminal," Grai said. "That way we don't have to waste time with trying to find someplace." He glanced at Carolina seated next to him then into the rearview mirror. "Grand Central is located at 42 Street and Park Avenue, and we will park less than a block away—200 Park Avenue." Mackenzie glanced at Dara and Jennifer, glad Grai had thought about where to park and had already done something about it. Jennifer flipped her ponytail, thinking the same thing. Dara continued looking out the window. For some reason she was picturing in her mind the complex system of Hoboglyphs, a secret language of symbols and codes used by transients in the 19th century.

The reserved space Grai had gotten was in a multi-deck, covered parking garage with valet service. Since it was obvious they weren't sure where they were going, Grai didn't wait to be invited. He went with them this time. Within minutes they arrived at what had been described as "the world's loveliest station and one of the nation's most historic landmarks." The sheer size was almost more than they could take in, as was the enormous crowd of people pressing in on them from every direction. "My gosh, this is like a village," said Dara. "How can we possibly find anyone at this location?"

"It's the sixth borough," said Mackenzie as she looked around, then, attacking the situation as a complex puzzle, she immediately devised a plan. "First of all, no matter what, we don't want to get separated," she said. "But, if we do, we will wait at the front entrance. Agreed?" Carolina, Dara, and Jennifer all nodded. Just then a large group of Japanese tourists came walking by—businessmen, more than likely, taking the day off to sightsee judging from the camera equipment they were all carrying. "Now, I think the number "61" figures into this somehow," continued Mackenzie, "so let's just canvass the area to see if that number shows up anywhere. What do you think, Dara?" Mackenzie looked around for her friend—"Dara?"— then suddenly filled with horror, "Where's Dara?" she screamed. Carolina immediately began yelling her name while Jennifer and Mackenzie searched nearby. Grai came running toward them from the direction of the main entrance. "What's wrong?"

"Dara has disappeared," Carolina told him, and she called out Dara's name again. People turned to look at the woman who seemed to be so frightened, but Carolina didn't notice.

"Maybe she had to find the ladies' room?" suggested Grai. But he knew that was lame. Dara would never have just walked off leaving the others and not telling them where she was going.

Carolina grabbed Jennifer and Mackenzie, wrapping her arms around them as though to protect them before they too would somehow be spirited away by forces she didn't understand. And even though she kept calling out Dara's name, she knew that it was too late—Dara couldn't hear her.

CHAPTER EIGHTEEN

"Can't you go any faster?" Larry asked the cab driver, unable to conceal his irritation.

"It's the cross-town traffic this time of day," the cabbie explained. "We'll get there, but it might take a while."

Larry impatiently ran his fingers through his hair. He shouldn't have let Carolina and the FIGs come to New York alone. He should have come with them. But he knew it wouldn't have mattered. There was nothing he could have done to remove the danger they were facing. But there might be now—assuming he could even get there.

"Turn left at the next corner and cut across to Park Avenue," he instructed the driver. That would at least get him within walking distance to Grand Central. The cab moved forward at a quicker pace for several blocks until it was forced to stop altogether. Larry could see Grand Central ahead. Jumping out of the cab, he quickly paid the driver and began running toward "the world's loveliest station and one of the nation's most historic landmarks."

***

Carolina was in tears. How could she have let this happen? Mackenzie and Jennifer held on to her, trying to come up with a plan but paralyzed with fear that something horrible had happened to their best friend and they would never see her again.

Grai pulled himself up to his full 6-foot height. "Listen, Carolina, I haven't intruded on what you have been doing these past few days. It wasn't my business. But now I think you need to tell me what's going on. I might be able to help, but you must trust me." He looked at the two FIGs clutching at Carolina's arm, imploring them. "Besides, if anything happens to one of you, Larry will be sure to call together a *kris* and insist on *marime*. I will be a disgrace to myself, my family, and to my tribe; and I will be banished." He smiled halfheartedly to give what he had just said some levity, but deep down he knew it could very easily happen. "I know it has something to do with a woman named Pearlee Devoraux Roux." He knew that because he had helped Larry trace her whereabouts in New York City. But Larry hadn't explained why he needed the information, and Grai hadn't asked. "Please, Carolina."

Trust him. He is a traveler. The words were clear. She nodded at Mackenzie and Jennifer, and the three started all talking at once, telling the man with one name about Dara who had been abandoned as a young child and was now trying to find her mother after ten years. They told him what they had learned so far—that Dara's mother couldn't have been at three of the addresses, but she had been at the fourth. "The man said she moved out about two or three weeks ago, and that she had a job working for the government in the city," provided Carolina. They told him about Mackenzie's grid with the "X" and Jennifer's strange image and musical notes. Then they told him about their trip to Frascati, the Voynich Manuscript, Mother and Papa Granchelli, Milosh—the wicked gypsy boy who placed the curse on Carolina, and the miraculous way she found her own mother.

"And Pearlee Devoraux Roux is her mother's name?" Grai asked when the conversation went full circle, back to where they first started talking about Dara who had been abandoned as a young child.

Carolina and the FIGs nodded.

Grai had already figured out quite a bit of what they were doing and why. And he had guessed it was Dara that it most concerned. But now he had more of the facts. This wasn't just a matter of trying to locate someone who had been missing for ten years, however. Something else was at play, and all of his instincts as a gypsy were telling him it was evil.

"Maybe we should just go to the authorities," said Carolina glancing around to see if there was a security officer nearby.

"I don't think that is wise, Carolina," said Grai. "We don't know what we are dealing with, but I don't think it is simply a matter of Dara being abducted."

All three young women got teary-eyed just at the mention of the word "abducted." Again, Grai presented the voice of reason. "Let's look at what we have. Mackenzie, you say the number "61" plays a part in this somehow. Right?"

Pulling on her inner strength as a Female of Intellectual Genius, Mackenzie tried to explain to him her reasoning by breaking down in simple terms the various formulae she had used in her calculations to pinpoint the exact location of Dara's mother at the Grand Central Terminal address.

"Okay. And Jennifer, you said the vision you have shows mostly gray and brown swirls, maybe like rocks, with a broad red streak and some yellow."

"That's right," she answered flipping her pony tail. "It is a broad, horizontal red streak, and the yellow is like a circle painted over the red."

"This might not make any sense—nothing about this does anyway—but... Through the decades of construction and renovation of Grand Central Terminal, one track remains a mystery. It is a secret track, Track 61, and it links Grand Central to the nearby Park Avenue Waldorf-Astoria, a hotel just five blocks away."

Carolina gasped.

"A publicly known connection between Track 61 and the Waldorf existed as early as 1929, but the rails never received much use. Track 61's first official use came in the transportation of General John J. Pershing in 1938, who, after a near-fatal heart attack, traveled cross-country in a weakened state to attend his son's wedding.

"After that, Grand Central Terminal authorities often kept a train car on Track 61 to handle emergency situations. FDR made use of the track at least once while in office. During this use, the train car on Track 61 held FDR's favorite automobile, and it could be opened to allow for the car to be driven directly onto the Waldorf-Astoria's freight elevator. In more recent times, security workers have found a lot of the homeless living on the train car and around the platform."

"How can we get to it?" asked Carolina.

"It isn't safe, Carolina. It has become a shadow world," Grai said, but even as he said the words, he knew they must go there if they were to have any hope of finding Dara.

"The only access to Track 61 now is past a guarded stairwell, as the freight elevator used to travel to the Waldorf-Astoria is welded shut. Theoretically, though, a train could be used on Track 61 today—the track would be a great way to leave New York City during an emergency." This last bit of information he seemed to be saying more to himself than to the others.

"We need to go there," said Jennifer.

"Right now," said Mackenzie.

Grai looked around. "I think I know how we might get past the guards. Follow me, but stay close." Grai pushed his way through the crowd and made his way to the outer perimeter of the main concourse. With Carolina, Mackenzie, and Jennifer following closely behind, he made his way past several specialty shops and restaurants. When he came to a door that appeared to be a utility closet, perhaps where cleaning supplies for the terminal were kept, he stopped. Ignoring the sign on it with the words "Staff Only" he backed up against the door and felt for the knob. It wasn't locked. "We need to be quick," he told the young women. "When I open the door, go through and wait for me." He glanced around the area waiting for the exact moment. A security camera above him slowly moved, scanning a section of the terminal near where they were standing. Another camera aimed in their direction from across the way paused, then slowly rotated to another area. "Now!" He quickly opened the door letting Carolina and the two FIGs enter. Just as quickly he closed it and waited as the cameras turned toward where he was standing, then again rotated to focus on other areas of the Terminal. In a few minutes, he also went through the door, quickly closing it behind him. He was standing in total darkness.

"Carolina?"

"We are over here," came her voice.

He felt along the walls until he reached the young women. "We need to walk about fifty feet straight ahead, away from the door where we came in. Then we should start seeing some dim light."

Slowly they felt their way through the darkness until coming to a narrow walkway lined with embedded low-density lights. They continued to follow Grai until they reached a stairway going down.

"Where are we?" asked Carolina as they descended. She wondered how he even knew so much about Grand Central. Overhead they heard the noisy grinding rumble of trains.

"The terminal itself covers an area of 48 acres, and the basement below that is 49 acres—from 42nd to 97th street. The platforms and tracks are on two levels, both below ground. We are beneath them."

They made their way down another flight of stairs, eventually coming to an area where the walls were actually bedrock. At one end of the large space there appeared to have been construction work going on, but was now stopped. "The MTA is in the midst of an ambitious project to bring Long Island Rail Road trains into the terminal via the East Side Access Project, making Grand Central even larger and deeper," explained Grai. "If they ever get it completed, these will be the deepest train tunnels on earth, at 90 feet below the Metro North track and over 150 feet below the street. It will take 10 minutes to reach these tunnels by escalator, at their deepest point."

"And you know all of this, how?" asked Jennifer, her question lost by the screechy, bumping movements of trains almost 100 feet above her.

Grai moved away from them as though getting his bearings. "We need to go farther north, under the Waldorf-Astoria. That's where the platform is and rail car "61." And the old freight elevator is there, too, but I doubt if would be operational even if it wasn't welded shut." Grai felt inside his pocket for the talisman he had kept with him since he was a small boy. It was there, a small, bright white stone. It gave him the reassurance he sought. "It's a pretty long walk. Do you think you can make it?" But he may as well have been talking to himself. Barely able to see, he led Carolina, Mackenzie, and Jennifer deeper into the bowels of the earth toward the danger and evil he knew existed in the other world hidden in shadows and darkness.

***

The crows gave warning first, then the starlings. The horse with the mark of the pentacle of Solomon on its forehead was the last to give notice to Lyuba that the settler was approaching. Lyuba went outside to wait. It was Lucia.

"Larry called," she said breathlessly as she rushed toward her friend. "He is at Grand Central Terminal in New York, and he needs to speak to you."

The two women went into Lyuba's hut where they could sit. "I saved his telephone number on my phone," she said even though she knew Lyuba wouldn't understand. She quickly dialed and then handed the phone to the gypsy when she heard it ring.

"Lyuba, I have searched everywhere I can think of—shops, restaurants, even where the trains are boarded, but I can't find them. Can you tell me anything else?"

Lyuba closed her eyes and envisioned the Tarot as she had placed them the evening before. Then she waited. Suddenly her eyes opened. "Larry, they are underground, deep underground. It is dark. They are going north. A traveler from another tribe is with them."

"Are there trains there, Lyuba? Because the platforms and train tracks are below ground."

"No, they are below the trains and tracks. They are below everything that is known."

"My god!" exclaimed Larry looking around. "How will I be able to find them?"

Lyuba began her chant, this time out loud. "Miseç yákhá tut dikhen/Sár páñ ori—/Mudaren!" ("Evil eyes look on thee/May they here extinguished be/And then seven ravens/Pluck out the evil eyes!) Larry shut his eyes, remembering from long ago when as a boy he had said the same chant that protected the child of a loving gypsy mother. Together they said it three times. When they finished, Larry knew he must not give up. If he had any chance at all to find them, he must face the danger.

Lyuba and Lucia sat together until early evening. Then Lucia returned to the farm to stay with Mother and Papa Granchelli rather than go to her own home. That way, she would be close by if she was needed.

***

Even though it was against her principles, and house rules, Mrs. Killebrew held up supper when Grai didn't return with Carolina and her three young women. When they hadn't arrived by 8 o'clock, she was truly concerned. Grai always called if he was going to be late. In fact the whole day had been strange, what with that phone call from someone she could hardly understand wanting to speak to Carolina. She didn't even know where the call was coming from until she looked up the area code. Somewhere in Italy of all places. Then she got that second phone call, this one from a woman she could understand who identified herself as Mrs. Ball from Wood Rose Orphanage and Academy for Young Women. What she wanted was to let Carolina know that she had given the first caller the phone number where she and the FIGs, she called them, were staying.

She wrapped up the left-overs and then went into the front room where she could watch for them to arrive. By 10 o'clock they still hadn't returned. Deciding she needed to do something, but not sure what, she called a neighbor who told her they were probably enjoying one of those New York dance clubs, and not to worry. But she knew better. Grai had never gone out at night—he simply wasn't that kind of person. And her guests, Carolina and those three young women—hadn't shown any interest in the New York night life either since arriving. Their interest involved something they needed to do during the day. After hanging up with her neighbor, she dialed the number Larry had given her in case of an emergency. When she got a busy signal, she left a message in his voice mail. Then she dialed the police department in the precinct where her boarding house was located.

CHAPTER NINETEEN

An explosion of what obviously was profanity, spoken in a variety of foreign languages and ancient dialects, reverberated throughout the dark tunnels. And although Dara couldn't see them well, she could smell the three men who were hustling her deep below the terminal, and the platforms and trains below that.

"Come on, missy, we ain't gonna hurt ya," one of the men said almost pleading.

The other man, who had a firm grip on her arm, said, "Someone wants to see ya. She's been waitin' for ya."

The third man didn't get a chance to offer anything since Dara once again let these abductors who were taking her who knows where against her will know exactly how she felt in the ancient dialect of the Romani New Indo-Aryan language with its Greek, Iranian, Kurdish and Armenian influences, something which she had been thinking about quite a bit since arriving in New York and the week before that at Wood Rose.

In addition to the foul odors emitting from the three men, there were other smells. Damp earth, oil, and staleness— something that reminded her of a construction site. The pathway grew narrow at one point so that they almost had to walk single file. Dara could feel the bedrock walls rub against her. Then the pathway opened up again. The surface they walked on was smooth—either hard compacted dirt or concrete, she couldn't be sure. There was light now, but very faint. Because it was what she had always done when confronted with insurmountable difficulties she focused on her private language. It was how her mind functioned. It was what made her a genius.

There were obscure scribbles and symbols on the dank, moldy walls that she could barely see. From what she could make out, she tried to establish the root of each main word, or symbol in some cases, and assign it a certain "weight" or number, trying to figure out the origin of the word. By knowing that, she would be able to recognize its meaning. It was her own system, something she taught herself as a young child. Only this time it didn't seem to work. The clouded scribbles and crude, murky embellishments were only gibberish.

"You need to know that I have a very good friend who is a gypsy, and she will put a curse on you and everyone you know or ever will know if you don't let me go—right now!" Again more profanity. "And not only that! You'd better hope there aren't any snakes down here, because if there are, she will put a double curse on you! Then you really will be sorry!" Even though Dara didn't like the fact that three homeless men had grabbed her at the Grand Central Terminal and were now taking her somewhere without her permission, she wasn't afraid. Because she was a Female of Intellectual Genius, she had known that something would happen over which she had no control when she saw Mackenzie's grid. In fact, she had more or less prepared herself to expect the unexpected. She just didn't expect this.

They reached some stairs and descended. After walking a few feet, Dara saw a light, although very dim, ahead. Now more curious than angry, she quit struggling as the three men escorted her toward the light.

***

The storm warnings were all around, and Lyuba had been especially watchful for their arrival. She greeted them when they at last came late in the night—tired and hungry, but glad they had finally reached the Old Villa. Her requests for the blessing of safe travel had been heard; her offerings accepted. The *Kaulo Camioes*—the Black Gypsies—had arrived safely. They would eat, then rest.

The next day, not wanting to waste any time in case the storm moved farther south than had been forecast, the gypsy women left early in the back of the old pickup truck to go to the village of Frascati where they strolled the streets, remembering the familiar and noting the unfamiliar from their previous visit, offering their wares. The men stayed behind to set up camp. Lyuba also remained behind, reading the Tarot. Just like no one questioned why she had left in the middle of the night to travel alone to the Old Villa, no one questioned her now, for she was the *choovihni*. There must be an important reason for it. Then right before dusk, when the last of the sun's rays—the crown of thorns she called it—were all that was visible on the western horizon, she visited the ancient live oak making her offering once again.

"There have been many changes since the last time we passed this way." The Bandoleer opened the conversation as they sat around the fire at the approach of evening discussing the day's events.

There were murmurs of agreement. "It is no longer a small village," one of the women said who had spent the day in Frascati. "We noticed it when we were here before."

"There are more people, but fewer want to buy," said another who had also spent the day trying to sell her services, but had little to show for it.

"There are many more strangers who have moved out of the cities." This from a woman who was disappointed to find her usual place where she had set up to sell her wares in the past was now a parking lot.

"We must be patient," said the Bandoleer. "There are many who don't know we are here yet. When they find out, they will want what we have to offer."

Lyuba remained in her hut while this discussion took place, reading her Tarot, gazing into her crystal, and preparing a mixture of ephedra and flitwort, healing herbs if used properly, but dangerous otherwise. Lucia had not returned which meant she had no further news. Lyuba would wait. *Be strong, my daughter.*

***

The sergeant on duty at the 33rd Precinct listened patiently to what Mrs. Killebrew told him, but he was quick to explain that until the people involved had been missing for twenty-four hours, she wouldn't be able to file a "missing persons report." Mrs. Killebrew was so insistent, however, and because, as she informed him, she always donated to the New York City Police Foundation, their Athletic League and all of their other various fund raisers, "and a considerable amount, I might add," he told her he would send over a couple of officers to talk to her first thing in the morning. Also, he noticed after checking the records, she had not called before, unlike many of the kooks who made a habit of calling once a month, usually when there was a full moon.

At the first signs of daybreak, two officers stood on the recently-swept porch with several rocking chairs, hanging ferns, and two concrete cherubs leaning against the newels of the steps. They didn't get a chance to ring the doorbell since Mrs. Killebrew had been watching for them from the living room. She quickly ushered them into her kitchen where they could sit at the table. She then poured them a cup of coffee she had brewed earlier that morning, right before sweeping the porch, that they could sip on while they wrote down notes about what she said.

"How well do you know this… Grai?"

"He has been living here for the past six or seven years or longer, and he is also a good worker," she answered. "And he isn't a night person, if that is what you are getting at."

"And what about these young women? You say they are renting rooms from you?"

"That's right. A former border made the arrangements. He is a professor at the University of North Carolina. He is also a friend of Grai's."

"And what are their full names?"

Mrs. Killebrew went into the living room and retrieved her register book that she required everyone to sign if they were a guest in her home. She showed it to the officers.

"What does FIG mean?" one of the officers asked.

"Well, that is what Larry—the university professor—called them when he made the reservation. I'm not really sure what it means."

The other officer set down his cup on the saucer that had been provided and looked at his partner. "Does that sound like a gang to you?"

"It isn't one I have heard of before. Maybe it is a new one."

"Gang?!" Mrs. Killebrew was mortified. "There are no gang members staying in my boarding house. Of all the stupid, idiotic… "

"We just need to consider everything," said the officer who first mentioned the word "gang" and was now sorry he had. "Well, I think that about does it. We have their descriptions you gave us, so we'll keep an eye out and let you know if we learn anything."

Mrs. Killebrew escorted the two uniformed men back out to the porch thinking that absolutely nothing had gotten accomplished by the officers coming over and not feeling the least bit better about the situation. She wished now she had asked more questions of the young women, but they had seemed so reticent, not really wanting to talk about what they were doing or where they were going each day. And Grai certainly hadn't been very informative or forthcoming either when she had questioned him. Besides, she didn't want to appear nosey. Gang! Really!

Walking back to their cruiser the first officer looked at his partner. "FIGs?"

"I think they might be that dangerous cartel that's come up from South America the Captain warned us about." Then he laughed. "She's probably just lonely and wanted some attention." He put away his notebook, his notes already forgotten.

***

"Why don't we stop here for a few minutes and catch our breath," suggested Grai. They had been walking for well over an hour and still had a long way to go.

Carolina and the FIGs didn't disagree. They were tired, but mostly they were worried. Each of them sat down on the hard surface next to the other, close enough where they would be touching, lost in her own thoughts.

Trying to make sense of where they were by translating it into mathematical equations, Mackenzie identified the construction around them as chevroned magic squares—N X N matrixes in which every row, column, and diagonal add up to the same number. But the fear of losing her friend was too great. Mackenzie started sobbing, and when she did, Carolina put her arm around her to comfort her.

The stone in Jennifer's chest had gotten large again. Flipping her ponytail, she fumbled around in her purse until she found a pen and a scrap of paper. The pain from the large stone was almost unbearable. There in the dim light, she began scribbling down musical notes into measures, phrases, and bars. The movements were now defined. When she had filled every blank space and there was no more room left on the paper, Grai pulled out a note pad from his pants pocket. "Will this help?" he asked offering it to her. Without saying anything, lost in her own world of musical *crescendos* and *accelerandos*, she quickly—urgently—continued writing down the notes on the blank pieces of paper. The more she wrote, the more its essence was revealed. It was a fugue in B flat minor with a prevailing ardent *leitmotif*, a musical composition in three movements—an exposition, a development, and a recapitulation that would return the theme back to the beginning in the fugue's tonic key. Contrapuntal in two voices, it was built on a single subject introduced at the beginning, then imitated at different pitches and connected by episodes through the course of the composition.

Over and over again Jennifer created the musical notations for *fortissimo* and *prestissimo,* loud and fast, on the staves she created with quick fervent slashes of her pen. Silently, Carolina and Mackenzie and Grai watched the young woman who had been a musical prodigy from the age of two draw the bass and treble clefs and fill in the notes. Then, at last, she stopped. She stared down at the sheets of paper scattered around her. "There is no recapitulation," she told the others quietly. "But there soon will be." Even though the others didn't understand, because they couldn't hear the notes, Jennifer heard them. And she understood that the two voices were Dara and her mother; the single theme was Dara's search for her mother. And when they found Dara, she would then know the notes for the recapitulation—the final entry of the theme, the musical return to the opening key of the fugue. When they found Dara.

***

No sooner had the police officers driven away, Mrs. Killebrew received a phone call from Larry letting her know that he was at Grand Central. If she found out anything, she could always reach him at the number he had given her. Then, somewhere between making up her bed and putting away the breakfast dishes, Mrs. Killebrew recalled a conversation—at least part of one—she overheard between Carolina and her three young women, and it had to do with Grand Central Terminal and "61." Being older, and having lived in New York City her entire life, she remembered that there had once been an old rail car used by Franklin D. Roosevelt, who tried to keep his paralysis from the public. If her memory served her, the number on the car had been "61." Of course, she had no idea if it was still at the Terminal somewhere, but could that have been what the four young women were interested in?

Not expecting squat from the two police officers—what a waste of time that had been—even after she gave them fresh coffee to drink, she went to the phone and dialed the number Larry had given her.

Frantic with worry, Larry had been scouring the terminal looking for any sign that would tell him what he needed to do or where he needed to go when his cell phone rang. It was Mrs. Killebrew. She quickly told him about FDR and the rail car, getting a little off the subject when she started talking about politics, only to be gently pulled back by Larry as to the reason for her call in the first place. "I'm fairly certain the number on the car was '61.' So you see, I just thought it might be something worth mentioning."

"The information you have given me is very helpful, Mrs. Killebrew. Thank you."

"Well... I am glad I could be of some assistance."

After ringing off, Larry immediately went to a security guard and told him that he needed to go to where the old "61" rail car was being kept. He also told Carlos, as identified by his badge, that it was a matter of life or death. Not sure of how to deal with the situation, Carlos took Larry to his boss, Antonio, and it was to him that Larry once again explained the situation and pleaded his case. Neither Carlos nor Antonio knew what to make of the story, and not only that, the area where the old rail car was located was strictly off limits to anyone. With the threat of terror, domestic, foreign, or otherwise, lurking behind every corner, strict rules had to be followed. But because Larry was the son of a Gypsy King, and because Lyuba was at that moment kneeling by the ancient live oak tree making her offering, they decided to make an exception and take this worried, passionate man past the guards and down the stairs to where old "61" was kept.

CHAPTER TWENTY

$\mathcal{T}$he nauseating smells of urine and rotting food was almost overwhelming, but, still, Dara kept moving through the dense, thick shadows of this ebony underworld toward the light. The sounds of breaking glass and rolling aluminum cans, moans and cries, and nonsensical babble penetrated her consciousness, but still she moved toward the light. No longer forcing her, the three men formed a flank around Dara, as though offering her protection. Up ahead, shadows began to take on shape and meaning; swirls of dense smoke and fog partially cleared and formed into tangible objects that could be identified. Then, suddenly, out of the darkness she saw it. An old rail car, painted red, with the number "61" painted in bright yellow on its side. She knew she had arrived where she was meant to be at that moment and in that place. She knew that was where she would find her mother.

***

Realizing she would never be able to concentrate at work, Lucia called her office letting them know she would be taking another day off. In fact, she had some vacation time coming, so she might just take a few days off. She stayed with the Granchellis through the morning, helping them with their chores. After all, it was better to stay busy rather than just sitting and worrying. But right after lunch she decided to pay Lyuba another visit. She could only imagine how worried she must be. Even though she had no additional information, at the very least these two women could give each other comfort. Walking through the deep grass she spotted a four-leaf clover. She would take it to Lyuba, for she had learned that such things had meaning, along with the basket of fresh eggs Mother Granchelli had sent.

By the time she reached Lyuba's hut, the gypsy was waiting for her and had already prepared tea for them to drink made with the root of the sassafras.

×**

With the musical composition Jennifer had scribbled down on the sheets of paper safely tucked away in her purse, Grai once again led the women through the dark subterranean cavern with nothing to guide them but his instincts. Up ahead, Mackenzie thought she could make out a large object of some sort, and there appeared to be more light as well. What sounded like someone throwing a glass bottle against the bedrock walls causing it to shatter startled the women. There were other noises now as well, not just the sounds of the trains moving on the tracks above them. "We aren't alone," whispered Grai.

Carolina and her girls clutched each other as they continued walking forward. Suddenly Mackenzie screamed. Carolina and Jennifer grabbed her and held on as something, someone was trying to pull her away from them. In this blackened world of nightmares where nothing seemed real, Carolina became aware that Grai was fighting whatever had hold of Mackenzie. When it finally let loose, the three women held each other terrified, unable to move.

"We must keep moving," Grai urged, his breathing heavy.

At one point Jennifer stumbled on something, causing her to drop her purse. When she felt around to find it, she realized what she had stumbled on was a body—human or animal, she couldn't tell. Carolina had already seen it as well as Jennifer's purse. She pulled Jennifer up along with her purse, and the two ran from the horror. Shuffling noises, at first only in front of them, were now all around them. "Don't stop," Grai warned, walking faster now. Carolina, Mackenzie, and Jennifer followed in terror.

***

Carlos and his boss, Antonio, had been down in the subterranean level only one time before, and that was when they had discovered that some homeless people were staying there. With the assistance of the New York Police Department, they had cleared them out, at least most of them, but that had been a while back. From the smell of things, no doubt they had come back.

"You still think your friends are down here?" asked Antonio, wondering why anyone would want to be there. He sure didn't want to be. He aimed his flashlight ahead in an attempt to give them as much light as possible. The area was so cavernous, however, and so dark, the light was virtually useless. He had heard stories about rats as big as Great Danes living down there. The last thing he needed was to come across something like that. He felt for his weapon and released the leather strap that held it securely in its holster.

"They are here," Larry said in answer to Antonio's question, for he knew. He noticed that Carlos had also released the strap that held his weapon in its holder. It sickened him to think that Carolina and the FIGs were there in that horrible place. And he was terrified because he knew the danger they were facing.

"Well, the rail car is over this way," Antonio said, pointing, "right under the Waldorf-Astoria." But something else had caught Larry's attention. In the darkness what had appeared to be the walls undulating were actually people. There were hundreds of them, hiding in every crevice and recess, cowering like wild animals, a lost society that had formed in this place of foul darkness. It was a shadow world of loss, despair, and hopelessness. If there was such a place as Hell, Larry thought, he had found it.

***

Because she believed that things always worked out for the best, and held firmly to the idea that positive action brought about positive results, Mrs. Killebrew decided to cook a nice hot meal for her guests. She just knew that Larry would find Grai and those young women, and that everything would work out. Since they had already missed the noon meal—dinner, she would bend the rules one more time and serve the noon meal for their supper. Besides, she had that nice pork roast she had been saving for a special occasion. Ralph, the butcher down the street who always cut her meats, had prepared it special for her, leaving just enough fat on it to give it a good taste. Holding onto those positive thoughts, she began pulling out cooking pans, dishes, cans, jars, and fresh vegetables from the refrigerator and pantry in preparation.

CHAPTER TWENTY-ONE

*E*ven as unimaginable horrors closed in on Dara, and the ragged broken sounds and rotten, putrid stench permeated her very soul, through the dimness of the light she was aware of only one thing: the tall woman standing at the back of the rail car with the red painted mouth. With their mission now completed, the three men stood aside, quietly waiting and watching. She had told them the girl would come one day, and that they needed to watch for her so they could let her know. That was their job, she had said. They hadn't failed. They had done as they were told. They had brought the young girl to the woman—their friend they called Pearlee.

"Mama?"

It was a small child's name for her mother—the one person in her life she had loved unselfishly and unconditionally with her entire being. Coming from the darkness of her memory, all of the raw feelings and torn emotions of hurt and pain hidden in that small child who had loved her mother so deeply only to be abandoned by her were now exposed in that one word.

With no more uncertainty, and no more guilt, Dara ran up the steps to the woman who had always called her "pretty girl." The woman who had sat with her on the back stoop of their rusted-out trailer whenever it flooded, while the ditch water lapped at their bare feet. The woman who burned kerosene in a big black pot to keep snakes away, and who had fixed her little girl's hair in big sausage curls the day she took her to the candy shop—and then left her.

The mother took her daughter in her arms and held her close. Sobs from the very depths of her soul spilled out in uncontrolled emotion. In that one single instant, the love, primal and basic,

130

that had been created in the womb and protected through all time by the birth, filled the loss and the distance that had existed so long between them. She had always known this moment would come. Her little girl was smart, and she knew one day she would look for her and keep looking until she found her. Now she had.

***

"We must go to the river," Lyuba told Lucia. "Hurry!"

Lucia followed behind the gypsy woman on the dirt path through the tall weeds that eventually ended in a thicket of trees next to the river. She watched Lyuba dig with her bare hands at the base of an ancient live oak tree and then remove what appeared to be a small parcel wrapped in paper. As she carefully unwrapped the paper, she began to chant. Still chanting she took the four-leaf clover Lucia had given to her from her pocket and placed it in the paper. After carefully wrapping it, she returned it at the base of the tree and covered it with soil. Lucia stood silently, knowing she was observing something sacred; something that very few settlers had ever been part of or witness to.

"Come with me," Lyuba said taking the other woman's hand. She led her down to the edge of the river bank where the water gently washed the soil and rocks, and where the tiny blue flower grew. Lyuba picked two, giving Lucia one to hold. Standing on the river bank, Lyuba once again chanted, holding the hand of the settler who had become her friend, knowing that Lucia's love for Carolina was pure and would, therefore, give added strength to her own love.

***

The sounds of evil were all around them, but Carolina heard other sounds as well. It was the voice of a *choovihni;* it was the voice of her mother. *You are in danger, my child. You must hurry. Run toward the big red box. Run!*

Unable to see in the darkness, with only her instincts as the daughter of a *choovihni* to guide her, she yelled to Mackenzie and Jennifer. "We must run!" And Grai followed, for he knew there was little time left.

***

Dara and her mother sat on a sofa covered in frayed damask silk woven in shades of gold and red and green, a remnant of grandeur and opulence from another time. "You were too young to understand back then," her mother explained. "But it was the only way I knew how to earn the money we needed to get by on." Dara thought back to the men who had come across the ditch bank dressed in their white starched uniforms; remembering how some of them had taught her strange, funny-sounding words from a foreign country, and how she learned to figure out which country the words came from. "Then one day a new man came with lots of ribbons and medals pinned on his uniform. He told me that some of the sailors had been telling me secrets— military secrets, and that I was going to prison because they couldn't trust me not to tell. Like I was a spy or somethin'." She looked at her grown daughter, seeing the little seven year old from all those years ago. "I hadn't done nothin' wrong, but they was goin' to send me to prison for something the sailors told me when they shouldn't have." She stroked Dara's hair and looked into her eyes, hoping she would understand. "They wouldn't have let me keep you. And I knew I couldn't take care of you if I didn't even know where I was goin' or how I was goin' to live. So I did what I thought was best. You were so smart. I knew you would be taken care of. But I was afraid to go to prison. So I just left." Tears spilled down her face as she squeezed Dara's hands. "It was the hardest thing I have ever done. You were my pretty girl. And I have regretted it all these years—that I wasn't able to tell you—to explain. How I couldn't let that man with all them ribbons and medals find me."

Dara nodded. At least now she knew why her mother had abandoned her. She didn't completely understand because in Dara's mind if you had a problem you faced it and did what you had to do to fix it. Running away wasn't an option. She looked at the woman who had given her life, recognizing those things from long ago that as a little girl she had loved—her mother; yet seeing other things that now with the passing of time were unrecognizable and different—a stranger. Dara glanced around trying to identify what the dim light would reveal. A couple of wooden chairs, an old chest, and strangely enough, a table with what looked like a telephone on it. "Is this where you live?" she asked, knowing that there was no job working for the government or anywhere else.

"It is—for now. And those men who brought you here are my friends. We take care of each other."

Dara thought of Mackenzie and Jennifer and Carolina. How they, too, took care of each other.

"You mustn't ever think that you did anything wrong," her mother told her. "You didn't. And you mustn't worry about me neither. You just keep doing good things, stay smart. You're my pretty girl. You always will be."

It started out as a soft bumping sound in a two-one sequence—just outside the rail car, but then it became louder. Dara's mother stood up and anxiously peered out of a dirt-encrusted window. "They are coming."

"Who?" asked Dara trying to see.

Her mother embraced her and held her child's face in her hands. There was so much she wanted to ask her daughter, but there was no time. "I must go. But remember what I told you. Do good things and stay smart."

"Who's coming?" Dara asked again, straining to see out the window. When she turned around, her mother was gone.

***

133

Grai heard it first, the bumping sound, and he knew it was some kind of warning—a signal within the fringe society. What he didn't know was if the warning was because of him and the women, or was it something or someone else. "We have to be getting close..." he told Carolina, but as soon as he spoke, someone grabbed him from behind and threw him to the ground. Not being able to see, he simply did what his instincts told him to do. Rolling to avoid the kicks and punches, grabbing at whatever hit him. Carolina screamed, and she held on to Mackenzie and Jennifer as they tried to run away from the horror. Up ahead they could just make out a rail car—red with the number "61" painted in yellow. "Run!" screamed Carolina, and the three young women ran toward the dim light of the rail car.

Just as they reached it, an explosion filled the air. "Was that a gun shot?" Mackenzie cried. Carolina didn't answer. She knew it was. Rather, she kept forcing her two charges toward the color red, praying that Grai hadn't been shot—or worse. Another gun shot rang out, this one from the direction where they had just come. All Carolina could think was that if they could just make it to the rail car, they would be safe. "Keep running!" she screamed. "Don't look back!"

The metal steps going up onto the platform of the car were steep and narrow, and Mackenzie slipped trying to climb up on them. Jennifer was right behind her, frantically pushing her friend, and Carolina followed, tripping and falling, desperately trying to get up the steps. When they reached the deck, Mackenzie pushed open the door and the three women rushed inside, slamming the door behind them. Fumbling around with the handle, Carolina found a bolt and shoved it, hoping it wasn't rusted beyond use. It slid easily, as though it had recently been used—securing the door. Exhausted, terrified, and hardly able to breath, Carolina, Mackenzie, and Jennifer stood trembling, holding each other, looking around at where they were, trying to comprehend. There in the dim light, on a sofa covered in frayed damask silk, a remnant from a by-gone era of wealth and opulence, sat Dara, alone, quietly crying.

CHAPTER TWENTY-TWO

*L*ucia felt a chill and shivered. Over and over again Lyuba repeated her chant, pleading, begging, imploring the fates to once again hear her cries and smile down on her precious daughter, protect her and those she loved—her girls. She squeezed the hand she was holding tighter, repeated the chant louder; for she knew. The terror Carolina and the FIGs were feeling, she was also feeling. The darkness Carolina and the FIGs saw, she also saw. Her breathing quickened to the point that she nearly collapsed, but still she held on to Lucia's hand.

Finally, at first barely discernable, then slowly, the dark cloud shifted, just enough to reveal a few of the sun's rays. It hesitated, then continuing on its course, it once again shifted, this time moving without pause until the sun's full brightness filled the sky. Its warmth comforted the two women. One, who had been partially responsible all those years ago for separating the child from her mother; the other, who had given the child life. Each from a different world, yet connected through their love for a young woman. They always would be. In the nearby thicket of trees, an owl hooted. It was a good omen.

***

Just as suddenly as the mob had attacked them, the mob disappeared, swallowed up by the dark blackness, unseen and unheard. Carlos returned his weapon to its holster, proud that he had been able to fire it into the air and scare away what undoubtedly would have been instant death for him, Antonio, and this man who was so determined to find his girlfriend and her students that he called the FIGs. Actually, it was the first time he had ever fired his weapon, and he felt quite exhilarated.

135

Antonio appeared out of the darkness pushing someone in front of him. "This guy didn't get away," he said.

Larry looked at him. "Grai?"

"Larry?"

"My god, are you all right?" Blood smeared his face and hands, and his clothes were filthy and torn. Fearing for the worst, Larry grabbed him, "Where're Carolina and the FIGs?"

"I told them to run when the mob attacked. We were trying to get to the rail car," he said pointing.

"You know this guy?"

"Antonio, this man is my friend. He was taking care of my girlfriend and her students. We have to get to the rail car."

The men took off running toward the red rail car that loomed ahead of them out of the darkness and into the dim light with a bright yellow "61" painted on its side.

***

Mackenzie sat close to Dara, feeling her pain, wanting to help but not knowing how, unable to say anything because she knew no one would be able to understand her. Jennifer merely stood quietly, tried to flip her ponytail, but her large blue eyes brimmed with tears instead. Carolina sat down next to Dara pulling Jennifer beside her, holding her hand. They would wait—together—until Dara was ready to tell them what had happened.

"Well, I found her," Dara said brushing the tears from her eyes.

Carolina nodded. "Your mother?"

"She lives here," she said looking around at the squalor. "Or, at least she did." Taking a deep breath, she tried to explain to her best friends something that was unexplainable. That her mother had entertained sailors when they were living in the back-bay area of Richmond, Virginia, in that old trailer. That was how she made her money so they could live. Then she told them the reason her mother had abandoned her, and why she was living as a fugitive.

"What about her job working for the government in the city?" asked Mackenzie.

Dara shook her head. "There is no job. She just made that up. The strange thing is, I think she is happy. At least she seems to be. You see, she has these three guys who are her friends." And she told them about the men who had taken her to her mother. "She told them I would come and to watch for me. Somehow she knew."

"Oh, Dara," Carolina put her arm around her and held her.

As Dara talked, Jennifer heard the remaining notes of the fugue, clear and defined. The final movement had at last revealed itself. The recapitulation had returned the theme back to the beginning in the fugue's tonic key. It was the final entry. And now it was complete. It was Dara's story, told in three chapters in B flat minor.

Dara's mother vanishes.

Dara searches for her mother and finds her.

Dara's mother vanishes.

She didn't need to write down the notes; she already knew them by heart—each note, each phrase, and each movement.

Mackenzie, needing now more than ever to be able to solve the problem—to somehow find the solution, grabbed her best friend's hand and squeezed it encouragingly. "We can find her again, Dara."

Dara smiled then. "I don't think she wants me to. And I'm not sure I want to either. I found out what I needed to know. That she loves me and she left me behind because she thought it was best for me. I'm all right with that. It's good enough. I don't need anything else."

Just then the bolted rail car door burst open crashing to the floor, and four men came stumbling into the room where Carolina and the FIGs were sitting.

"Larry! Where did you come from? Grai?"

"Are you all right?" Larry pulled Carolina up as though uncertain she wasn't an apparition of some sort and then embraced her. "I was so afraid for you—for all of you." He held

Carolina away from him making sure she was there and in one piece, then pulled her close to him again.

Grai, cut, bruised, and looking a lot worse for wear, smiled at each of the FIGs, happy that they were all accounted for and appeared to be safe, yet still trying to convince himself that they were in fact all there and nothing had happened to them under his watch.

Carlos and Antonio simply stood back and grinned. This was good. The passionate young man had found his girlfriend and the three young women called the FIGs.

Because Dara was the tallest and the most aggressive of the FIGs, she spoke first. "Let's get out of this place!" With Carlos and Antonio safely leading them back to the guarded stairs, they ascended out of the darkness and into the brightness of "the world's loveliest station and one of the nation's most historic landmarks."

CHAPTER TWENTY-THREE

"They have many goals ahead of them," Carolina said in answer to Mrs. Killebrew's question about what the FIGs planned to do now that summer was almost gone. "Dara has been accepted at Yale University on a full scholarship. She wants to continue her studies in foreign languages and perhaps at some point go into the diplomatic service. Mackenzie, who you have probably noticed is a whiz at math, has been accepted into the Massachusetts Institute of Technology research program. An anonymous donor and Miss Alcott, one of our financial supporters at Wood Rose, are sponsoring her. I'm not sure where Mackenzie will land. Her problem-solving abilities spill over into human relationships as well. She is a peace-maker. I think she will be able to do whatever she decides she wants to do. And Jennifer will attend Juilliard when she isn't actually performing. She has already been received by the international world of music. Now they are just waiting for her reintroduction." They had finished eating Mrs. Killebrew's roast pork and everything else she had fixed to go with it, as well as the apple pie she had baked that was big enough to feed everyone at Wood Rose—"just a little something I whipped up"—and it was just Carolina and Mrs. Killebrew and Larry remaining at the table. The others— Dara, Mackenzie, and Jennifer—had excused themselves to go upstairs. Grai had also turned in early after Mrs. Killebrew had doctored his cuts and bruises—fussing at him all the while— and after he had eaten double portions of everything, at Mrs. Killebrew's insistence.

Larry would spend the night at the boarding house, but then would return to Chapel Hill the next day to resume his teaching duties and catch up with the tardy student who had to reschedule his appointment.

Much to Mrs. Killebrew's delight, Carolina and the FIGs would remain a while longer. "We really haven't had a chance to see much of the city, other than that quick tour Grai took us on the first day we arrived." So they would stay until after the performance of Jennifer's symphony, *The Gypsy Cadence*, at Carnegie Hall. And, they would meet with Dr. Pedigrew at the Beineke Library. Then they would return to Wood Rose Orphanage and Academy for Young Women in order for the FIGs to pack up their personal things—what few things they had—before going to the universities where they had been accepted.

Earlier in the evening, Mrs. Killebrew told Carolina of the two unusual phone calls she had received: one from a woman in Italy, who left no message; the other from Mrs. Ball at Wood Rose Orphanage and Academy for Young Women, who left the message that she had given out the phone number where Carolina and the FIGs were staying at the boarding house to a woman named Lyuba. And that it was important. Carolina had to smile. She could only imagine the grief Headmaster Harcourt had given Mrs. Ball for giving out any information like that since it was strictly forbidden. Later, after everyone else was asleep, Carolina dialed the number in Italy. She didn't need to look it up; she knew it by heart. It was the nearest thing she had to being able to connect with her mother. Even though it wasn't even daybreak there, she knew they were together waiting in Lyuba's hut to hear from her. She would call Mrs. Ball a little later in the morning—before the headmaster got to his office—to thank her.

"Carolina!" Lucia cried. "I have been so worried, but Lyuba said you were all right. And the FIGs?"

Carolina reassured her that she was all right, as well as the FIGs, and everything was fine.

"Your mother wants to talk to you," Lucia said filled with emotion and obviously overjoyed that Carolina had called.

For the next several minutes mother and daughter shared their love for one another across the miles. There was no need to discuss the events of what had taken place. Lyuba already knew, just as she knew that Carolina had heard the warnings she had sent. Because her daughter had the gift.

When Carolina ended the call, she quietly went from room to room, first checking on Dara, the bed sheets neatly folded around her, then Mackenzie with her foot sticking out from the crumpled covers like a barometer, then Jennifer, with sheets of eight-stave paper scattered across her bed. Satisfied that they were safe, she returned to her room, knowing they still had some unfinished business to take care of and so much to look forward to.

***

With all of that trouble about the phone call now behind them, a new problem seemed to present itself to Mrs. Ball and Headmaster Harcourt. Insidious, intangible, but nonetheless very real, a feeling of dejection seemed to invade the atmosphere of Wood Rose Orphanage and Academy for Young Women and fill every nook and cranny—like some noxious gas. Everyone residing and working within the ivy-covered stone walls of Wood Rose sensed it and seemed to be affected by it—although some more than others. And the symptoms varied from person to person as well, from some feeling slightly irritable to others developing a state of full-blown manic depression.

It was with a feeling that lay somewhere between cantankerousness and sadness that Mrs. Ball unlocked her office door and flipped on the lights, only to be startled out of her wits to find Miss Alcott sitting in the dark on the dark green sofa in Headmaster Harcourt's office. Feeling more irritable than depressed, Miss Alcott apparently had let herself in, as she had every right to do as the great niece of Wood Rose's founding father and active member of the Board of Directors, and was simply "sorting some things out and thinking things through" as she saw them. It wasn't long before Mrs. Ball joined Miss Alcott on the sofa so she too could sort some things out and think them through, and that was where the headmaster found them, sipping tea, when he arrived a short while later.

"You are nothing but a pompous stuffed shirt," accused Ms. Alcott, whose well-known acid tongue and strong opinions had reddened the headmaster's ears with regularity over the years. She glared at his conservative dark gray suit and his equally conservative gray-striped tie. "It's just too quiet and boring around here without Carolina and her girls," she told him, "and you run this place like a funeral parlor!"

She was right. It was too quiet—and too boring. Not only that, as difficult as it was to admit, he was a pompous stuffed shirt. And even the appearance of the soft blush of red tips on his prize *Photinia frasen* couldn't alter that fact. Mrs. Ball sipped her tea refusing to make eye contact with her boss. She agreed with Miss Alcott; after all—he was a stuffed shirt, and it was much too boring without the FIGs and Carolina on campus to keep things stirred up. "And now they will soon be gone," continued Miss Alcott. In spite of everything, she had enjoyed hearing about the expressions of creativity the FIGs had managed to achieve over the years at Wood Rose. It had made her feel young again. In fact, they reminded her just a bit of when she was their age, only the "childish pranks," as they were called back then, that she and her friends played were on a much smaller scale and not nearly as creative. It just wouldn't be the same with them gone. She peered dejectedly into her cup of tea.

"Of course Ms. Lovel will still be here," Headmaster Harcourt offered with a weak smile and not much enthusiasm. But he knew what Miss Alcott meant. Wood Rose would probably never again enjoy the experience of having a female of intellectual genius as a resident/student on campus, let alone three at the same time. In fact, he was positive no other campus in the world had ever had such an experience.

He had been envious at first of Carolina and her ability to connect with the FIGs, but now was just grateful that she had come along when she did. The respect and affection the FIGs felt for her was more than a little evident. She had been able to give them something that no one else on campus had—including himself. Thankfully, she would remain at Wood Rose to teach, but it would seem strange not to have the FIGs around, and, as Miss Alcott pointed out, much too boring. He sighed deeply and plopped down in his black leather chair behind his desk, cringing slightly as he remembered the recent episode of the missing light bulbs.

"Well, you obviously haven't given it much thought," admonished Ms. Alcott still on her rant, "but I have." And she proceeded to tell the headmaster and his secretary what she planned to do. It wouldn't change the fact that the FIGs were leaving Wood Rose, but at least, temporarily, it would ease their pain of no longer having them around.

CHAPTER TWENTY-FOUR

For the next three weeks, Carolina and the FIGs divided their time between exploring all of the wonderful places in New York City that Grai knew about, and Jennifer's rehearsals. Larry was able to join them for a few days between summer school sessions, and whenever the question came up about Mackenzie's grid—the four red dots forming a perfect square with Grand Central Terminal indicated by the "X" in the middle—they could only shake their heads and shrug it off. "It is just one of those unexplained universal cosmic things," said Larry. "Just like when Carolina decided it was time to go to Frascati, Italy, not knowing that her mother would also be there at that exact same time with her tribe. Or how three young girls with intelligence quotients in the genius range from different parts of the country could all wind up at Wood Rose Orphanage and Academy for Young Women. Some things just can't be explained."

Continuing with that line of reasoning, Carolina and the FIGs also decided not to question Grai about why he chose to drive a cab driver in New York City when he was obviously well educated and could do other things if he chose to; or how he was able to take so much time off in order to drive them around the city. As Larry said, there were some things that just couldn't be explained, nor did they need to be.

As the days grew shorter and the temperatures got a little cooler heralding in the change of seasons when summer would end and autumn would begin, there was another change that seemed to be taking place in the minds of Carolina and her girls. Brought on from the realization that each FIG would soon be going her separate way, a quiet, unspoken and pervasive melancholy seemed to overshadow the last, happy, carefree days of summer. Carolina and the FIGs had gone through so much together; their bond of understanding and trust had never been stronger or their love for each other greater. Lurking in the darkness of their subconscious thoughts, however, was the fearful inevitability that they would meet with other difficulties and obstacles in life. Challenges that they had no way to predict. This created feelings of uncertainty for the FIGs as well as Carolina, because, being separated, each going to a different university—or in Carolina's case, she would have new responsibilities at Wood Rose that didn't include her girls—they weren't sure how they would overcome those difficulties and obstacles as individuals—separate and alone—because they were Carolina and the FIGs. Together, and not separate.

When the evening arrived for the sold-out premiere performance of *The Gypsy Cadence,* with Jennifer playing principal first violin, the much sought after choice seats—center parquet B section of Carnegie Hall—were occupied by Carolina, Mackenzie, and Dara, along with Larry, Grai, and Mrs. Killebrew. In addition, also seated in the choice seats, Headmaster Harcourt, Mrs. Ball, and Miss Alcott had made the trip from Raleigh, North Carolina, as representatives of Wood Rose Orphanage and Academy for Young Women. Arranged and paid for by Miss Alcott, it was the least they could do to offer their support to one of their most brilliant graduates. It was also their way of coming to grips with the knowledge that the FIGs would soon be leaving Wood Rose for good.

Following the stellar performance that included numerous encores, a brief rendition of Jennifer's beautiful piano sonata she had first performed at age thirteen, and standing ovations that seemed to go on forever, rumors began circulating throughout the concert hall that Jennifer had recently completed another masterful piece of music as well—a fugue titled *The Wish Rider.* And when Andrew Whatley, Director of Special Events at Carnegie Hall, confirmed those rumors with an announcement, Mrs. Ball, Miss Alcott, and the headmaster of Wood Rose immediately made plans to attend that performance as well once they knew when it was to be scheduled.

A few days later Carolina and the FIGs met with Dr. Pedigrew, head of special research projects at the Beinecke Library at Yale, to discuss their findings regarding the letter Carolina's father had written to her when she was born and its similarity to the Voynich Manuscript, the most mysterious document in the world. When they left, it was with Dr. Pedigrew's heart-felt enthusiastic assurance that the report the FIGs had prepared from their research of the Voynich while in Frascati, Italy, would be published in the upcoming issue of the university's prestigious journal.

Everything they had set out to accomplish at the beginning of the summer was now completed, and Carolina and the FIGs returned to Wood Rose. With only two days left before Dara, Mackenzie, and Jennifer were to report for orientation at their new schools where they would be attending, and Carolina would start teaching young female students in regular classes at Wood Rose that did not include her girls—the FIGs, the anxiety that had been hidden in their subconscious thoughts moved to the forefront of their conscious thoughts enveloping the four young women in a dark black funk.

"We can always see each other over the holidays," Dara reminded the others.

"Yeah, but where? I mean, it's not like any of us has a home to go to or anything," said Jennifer, flipping her long blond ponytail, "except for Carolina."

"Yeah," agreed Mackenzie. "I don't think they even allow students to stay on campus over the holidays at MIT," her lisp pronounced as she wondered where she could go and all of the stressful difficulties that brought about.

Carolina jumped into the discussion that they had been having over coffee—with sugar for Mackenzie and cream for Dara and Jennifer—in her one-bedroom bungalow with the brightly colored, hand-sewn cushions and slip covers and pretty damask draperies. "That is absolutely no problem. All of you will come and stay with me!" She saw the looks on their faces as they glanced around and considered the smallness of her living space. "Right, it might be a little tight, but the sofa pulls out and sleeps two. And my bed sleeps two. We shared the one bathroom at Mrs. Killebrew's boarding house and managed fine. We will have a good time! This is your home!" she said emphatically.

"Well, we do have other options," said Dara. "We could *all* go visit Mother and Papa Granchelli," placing major emphasis on the word "all."

"Or we could go stay with Mrs. Killebrew again," suggested Jennifer.

"Or we might want to go to a completely different place—a place we've never been to before," added Mackenzie, suddenly feeling a little better—even adventurous. What she didn't say was something she had been mulling over a lot ever since getting back from New York. Something that she hadn't even mentioned to Dara or Jennifer or Carolina yet because she was still thinking about the numbers she had assigned to it and creating the corresponding formulae and equations and even a special chart using the Talagrand concentration inequality theory. And that was—maybe—if Larry could find out anything, no matter how small or insignificant, just maybe they could search for her parents. But she still needed to think about it a little more, play with her numbers and equations and formulae and, of course, that chart, before actually talking about it out loud.

"There, you see," said Carolina. "That gives us all kinds of possibilities."

Gradually, in tiny hesitant increments, the dark funk began to be replaced by small white glimmers and tiny sparks of light until finally disappearing altogether. And, as Carolina pointed out to them, repeatedly and with a great deal of fervor, they had so much to look forward to. Not only that, the first school break was only a few weeks away, which meant they would be seeing each other again very soon.

Late that night—the "witches' moments," the last night they would spend in the dormitory, in their three-bedroom suite located on the second floor at Wood Rose Orphanage and Academy for Young Women, three young women—Dara, Mackenzie, and Jennifer—tiptoed barefooted across the wide expanse of lawn wet with glistening dew, shadowed with tall pines and massive oaks draped in Spanish moss, and slightly illuminated by the crescent moon overhead, from the direction of the administration building, lugging a long ladder and some hedge clippers, making their way to the Alcott Chapel. Once there, they dropped the ladder and the clippers, creating a noisy clatter that was followed by a burst of giggles, and quietly pushed open the ornate doors. Inside, Dara, with the top two buttons of her pajama top unbuttoned and the legs of her pajama bottoms rolled up, aimed her flashlight toward the large portrait of Miss Alcott hung next to an equally large portrait of her Great Uncle Horace, both done in oils, in the vestibule above a Queen Ann console table. Mackenzie, with all of her pajama buttons closed and the legs slightly wet at the bottoms because she chose not to roll them up, aimed her flashlight toward the center of the table where a large Waterford crystal vase filled with fresh pink roses had been placed, the pink roses complimenting the pale pink color of the garment worn by Miss Alcott in the portrait. Flipping her ponytail, Jennifer, who had decided not to wear pajamas but rather a night shirt that had the hem rolled up into a bulge and tied in a knot just below her hips, grabbed the fresh roses and dumped them unceremoniously into the large silver collection plate that got passed around each Sunday for donations. Then, reaching into the bulge in her night shirt she pulled out fresh cuttings from the beautiful prize *Photinia frasen,* the magnificent red-tip bush the FIGs had named *Peni erecti* that grew in front of Headmaster Harcourt's office window, and stuffed them into the large crystal vase, angling the vase so that it was perfectly centered.

"That looks much better," said Dara causing a fresh explosion of giggles. "Let's get out of here." Outside, once again grabbing the ends of the ladder, Dara and her two best friends hauled it and the clippers back to the shed that housed the lawn maintenance equipment. Task accomplished, their creative expression expressed, they returned to their suite, and to their individual beds, careful not to disturb the other dorm residents, the floor monitors, and, most importantly, their slumbering dorm mother, Ms. Larkins. Within minutes, they fell into a deep, peaceful sleep—the sleep of innocent angels.

It would soon be light; and Wood Rose Orphanage and Academy for Young Women would start another day.

The Clock Flower Project –
Book 3 of The F.I.G. Mysteries

Carolina tearfully watched the plane carrying her girls away as it nosed into take-off position. She slowly lowered the sign she had made for the occasion—**SEE YOU IN 108 DAYS**.

Her girls—

Dara Roux, abandoned when she was seven years old by her mother. Exceptionally gifted in foreign languages. Orphan.

Mackenzie Yarborough, no record of her parents or where she was born. Exceptionally gifted in math and problem-solving. Orphan.

Jennifer Torres, both parents killed in an automobile accident when she was sixteen. Exceptionally gifted in music and art. Orphan.

The three FIGs—Females of Intellectual Genius—as they were called at Wood Rose Orphanage and Academy for Young Women, probably couldn't even see the sign, but holding it made Carolina feel a little better about everything. It kept them connected just a little while longer.

As the plane began picking up speed down the runway, Larry put his arm around her, sensing how she must be feeling. "They will be fine," he reassured her for the umpteenth time since early that morning. Even though it meant getting one of his teacher's aides to take over his morning class at the university, he had volunteered to take Carolina's three students to the Raleigh-Durham airport and be with Carolina to see them off.

Carolina watched the plane lift off the ground and point toward the sky. On an impulse, she waved and once again held up her sign until the plane disappeared from view. Then she burst into sobs. Larry knew it was coming. He wrapped his strong arms around this woman he loved and held her, knowing that was all he could do. As the son of a gypsy king, he knew that words simply wouldn't help.

The past year had been an unbelievably strange journey for them beginning when Carolina was hired to be totally responsible for three "incorrigible," as the headmaster described them, teenage girls their final year at Wood Rose: all three orphans with intelligence quotients in the genius range. Being only a few years older than the FIGs, she immediately filled the role of a big sister and friend to them. As far as the FIGs were concerned, she was their Carolina; she was one of them. And with everything that they had experienced in that brief time they had been together, a bond had been forged and their lives would be forever intertwined.

It all started with finding Carolina's birth mother in Italy—a gypsy. Then there was the deadly curse that was placed on Carolina, which eventually led to the connection between a letter she had inherited and the most mysterious document in the world—the Voynich Manuscript.

And then, only a few weeks later, they located Dara's mother in New York City, hiding underground beneath Grand Central Terminal where she lived in some sort of secret subculture with three homeless men. It was remarkable, really, and something that only the FIGs and Carolina could have accomplished. Through it all, Larry had been there for them, offering his support and using his innate instincts as the gypsy king's son to gather information that would help them.

Larry held Carolina tighter as her sobs quieted. He would tell her later what Mackenzie had asked him to do just before boarding the plane. After he had a chance to see what he could find out.

As the plane reached cruising altitude, shoulder bags placed under the seat in front of them within easy reach, Dara, seated between Mackenzie and Jennifer, as usual was the first to say out loud what each of them was thinking.

"OK, this is what I think we ought to do." She glanced at her two best friends to make sure she had their attention. "We will give this 'pursuit of advanced studies' a try, even though it means being separated. But if things don't work out by winter break—for any one of us—then I say we come up with another plan. A plan where we can be together. Deal?"

"Exactly!" said Jennifer.

"Agreed!" said Mackenzie.

With that simple declaration—an oral commitment made between three Females of Intellectual Genius—the stress of what was happening to them, the realization that their lives were about to be forever changed, was made more acceptable. They could survive knowing that there was an out, and the option that they could be together again would always be there for them. With their biggest concern now addressed, each FIG settled back to concentrate on what was ahead.